Chapter One

"So, I want you guys to imagine. Imagine 100 billion of our suns in just our galaxy alone. Can you picture how big that is?!" Ethan raised his voice in an excited fashion toward his 11th grade students. His arms froze, outstretched, ready for an embrace – an embrace of mutual passion for the science he devoted a large portion of his life to. His arms closed to his sides again and his voice briefly relaxed.

"Let me try to put that in perspective," he continued. "The closest star to us is over four light years away. Light can circle the Earth seven and a half times in one second. Seven and a half times in *one second*!" Ethan's eyes and eyebrows climbed along with his voice.

"The distance light goes in over four years is how far the *closest* star is to us," he sternly went on. "So, again, 100 billion of these stars are in our galaxy, the Milky Way."

A dramatic pause.

The 28 students sat behind their desks listening intently, but not yet in awe with what they had just heard. It was a good group of teenagers. None of them really were mischievous in that physics classroom. They may have been in a different classroom environment – maybe English Literature or American History or something of the like. But not there. These kids showed actual respect for their instructor, which was rare in the California public school community. These students could see their teacher, Mr.

Ethan Pleate, had a vast knowledge bank and was not only unafraid to share it with others, but he strove and went out of his way at times to do so. Not only that, but he also genuinely cared about his students' education. Mr. Pleate constantly reminded his students he was available any time of the day to help with any type of problem or concern, be it a math problem, an art class project difficulty, a problem with a girlfriend, something wrong at home or even a Spanish class problem. He was there for anything – except for Economics class. He didn't care for economics. And because of this devotion to his job and its surroundings, Ethan Pleate's class reciprocated – even if the students weren't as passionate about the actual teaching material as the instructor.

Ethan dipped his head down to gather his thoughts. His eyebrows scrunched, his eyelids squinted down, his breathing got deeper and he began to pace around in a small circular path. He shot his arms out in front of him to bring his already half-way rolled up sleeves just a bit higher, exposing two strange tattoos on his forearms.

The tattoo on his inner left forearm was of a carbon atom, with each particle about the size of a quarter. The electrons were depicted with rotation marks and they each spun the same direction. He wanted to show his fascination with the concept of quantum entanglement.

Quantum entanglement is a rather strange phenomenon which shows how particles can be mutually connected without physical attachments to one another and despite the distance between them. If a force is acted upon one of these connected particles that causes a change to it, then that same change is felt on the other particle, even if the latter is 10 billion light years away, in a vacuum, with nothing remotely close to it. It is a bit like taking a mother's sixth sense toward her son to the next level.

The other tattoo was drawn on his inner right forearm. It is a unique and oddly beautiful interpretation of the inner workings of a four-dimensional star. It looks nothing like the normal stars most people are familiar with. This one doesn't have four, five or even eight different points; this one has countless points which don't seem to even have a pattern. It looks like a star *bush*, with a core of points and branch-like arms that sprout other pointed masses. The shading is what makes the tattoo artistically beautiful. The meaning is what makes it intellectually beautiful: it acknowledges that there is more to our lives and universe than what we can actually see. It accepts the possibility of more dimensions than just the three we humans can see. Our current quantum physics concept of string theory allow for more dimensions, more 'universes', and limitless possibilities. That is just awesome.

These tattoos lay half-exposed beneath a bright red tailored dress shirt. Mr. Pleate needed to have all his shirts tailored because of his slim physique. Any store-bought collared shirt would look like a dress on him. And it was very important for Ethan Pleate to have a collared dress shirt, tie and slacks while at work. He felt he needed to be professional and look professional at work. After all, it was work, not home. He always kept a shaved hair cut, shaved moustache and beard, and even remarkably clean lenses on his glasses. That day, the red shirt was matched with a bright yellow and gold tie that had pin stripes going diagonally down. These both looked great with black slacks.

One foot stepped out in front of the other, continuing a circular track as Ethan's arms went back to cross in front of his chest. He took a big breath of air to add emphasis and dramatization to his next words, "Now I want you to imagine 100 billion *galaxies*."

A pause and another contemplative look to the floor.

"A hundred *billion* galaxies. Each containing about 100 *billion* stars. Most of these stars having planets going around them. I say most because pulsar stars are thought to not contain orbiting planets. *But*, we *have* confirmed planets going around a pulsar. Not only a pulsar, but a binary of pulsars."

Again, Ethan Pleate had an uncontrollable tangent.

"If you guys don't remember what a pulsar is, it is the remnants of a supernova explosion."

A smile grew on Ethan's face, excited simply because he enjoys discussing the subject. Just like a young boy discussing his favorite Hot Wheel toy cars to his friends, Ethan's face lit up and his voice turned faster and slightly louder.

"These super dense, super bright stars are about the size of a large city, but weigh as much as our sun. They spin incredibly fast. Some of these pulsars can make hundreds of revolutions in under a second. And they keep this amazing speed for a very long time. People can actually use these pulsars as the best clocks ever imaginable because of how long they keep their constant spin."

Mr. Pleate was beginning to ramble and he knew it. He shook his head from side to side to get his thoughts back on track. But his voice was still quick and energetic.

"Uh, anyways. 100 billion stars in a galaxy with 100 billion galaxies in the universe. That's a lot of planets, stars, gases and space."

Ethan looked around at all the faces in the class. They didn't seem to be as awestruck as he was. The students didn't seem bored or confused, either, though. It was a simple mathematical problem: 100 billion stars multiplied by 100 billion galaxies equals the total amount of stars in the universe. So what's the big deal? That was the question staring back at Ethan.

"Okay, well, that's a whole lot of stuff," Mr. Pleate scientifically explained as he stood in a more composed manner, drawing back the unaccepted energy he had just thrown out.

In the blink of an eye, the thrill shot back into him. He took a deep breath and held up his right arm with his its fingers spread wide, facing downward, as if he were palming an invisible basketball.

"Alright, if that doesn't boggle your mind, check this out..."

His eyes went toward the ceiling to add effect and to show importance in what he was about to say.

"Everything in our universe – all of those stars, planets, gases, galaxies – every single little atom that makes up all of those things, came from a single source smaller than the point of a needle 13.6 billion years ago."

Ethan paused again, expecting to hear gasps of amazement. But silence prevailed.

"Every single thing we can see here, around the world, through telescopes," Ethan had a tendency to repeat himself over and over, maybe a way for his students to fully understand the nature, "came from a singularity smaller than an atom."

Ethan froze in an exaggerated, flamboyant pose, waiting for some sort of response from the audience.

Seconds later, a response came in the form of a ringing bell, signaling the end of the seventh and last period of the day.

Chattering had begun as the rustling of papers, books and bags filled the classroom. Mr. Pleate squeezed in his usual end-of-class last words.

"Okay, get out of here, guys and girls," he said in a loud voice to overcome all the hustle. "And remember, if you guys need help with anything at all, come see me at any time."

Ethan stood with a smile, facing his students with his hands now resting in his pockets. He never sat down or turned away or left his class until every last student was out of the room – unless, of course, it was all part of his act. He was always attentive to his students and wanted to show them he was always ready to help them out. He never wanted to show he was not 'working'.

Students started vacating the room. "Goodbye"s, "see ya later"s and "take it easy, Mr. Pleate"s were being directed towards the front of the class as a small bunch of teenagers was forming at the narrow doorway.

One student began to make her way towards Mr. Pleate. It was one of Ethan's better students, Astrid. She was a very pretty young girl, with long, silky black hair. Her Indonesian parents had given her dark eyes, dark skin and a small frame. She often proudly wore her culture's traditional Batik clothing. It is a style that portrays mostly darker colors, especially browns, in very unique patterns, somewhat resembling paisley. That day was no exception. She wore a Batik top with jeans and sandals.

She reached Ethan and hesitantly said, "Mr. Pleate, I have a personal problem that I want to see if you can help me with."

"Ya, sure thing, Astrid," Ethan said in a comforting way.

Astrid looked back to confirm the last student had left. She turned her head back at Ethan.

"Mr. Pleate, I have a problem with my boyfriend," she began to explain. "My boyfriend and I have been going out for like six months. And he's at the point where he really wants to have sex. But I'm a very traditional girl and I don't think I'm ready for it. And to tell you the truth, I'm a little scared."

I know what you're thinking: 'Why the hell would this young girl go to her physics teacher to seek help about relationships or sex?' Again, Mr. Pleate was no ordinary physics teacher. He was more like an older best friend. His openness and his caring nature led to his students not only becoming his tutees, but becoming his friends.

Mr. Pleate often talked about his personal life, interests, feelings and opinions. He knew, of course, where to draw the line. He didn't ever discuss his love life. But astonishingly, he did even discuss his views on politics and religion and other sensitive topics. Many people avoid these because they don't really know how to talk about them. Mr. Pleate knew how. Even though he had 'radical' views, Ethan read people very well and was able to realize when a conversation was getting too heated. When that happened, he would skillfully steer the discussion into a different path. And it was this openness and information-revealing method that allowed Mr. Pleate's students to get to know the true person. Just like true friends know one another, Ethan Pleate and his students held almost nothing back.

"It's okay to be scared, Astrid," Mr. Pleate delivered. He made himself more relaxed and informally sat on a long table at the front of the room. "Everyone is scared their first time with their partner. Even if a person is very experienced, their first time with a new partner can be frightening."

He continued, "What I think you should do is wait until you are totally comfortable with the idea of sex and wait until you are truly ready. You don't want to regret something when you can avoid it completely."

Astrid curiously listened and studied the words coming out from Ethan.

"And when you are one million percent sure you are ready for sex, take it slow and easy. Make sure you communicate to your boyfriend if something hurts or if you are uneasy in any way. The most important thing is you and your comfort."

Ethan formed a soothing smile and laid his right hand on Astrid's left shoulder.

"But remember: if you're not ready, you're not ready. Don't force anything."

Astrid let out a bright smile, showing her beautiful, gleaming white teeth and replied, "Thanks a lot, Mr. Pleate!"

"Ya, sure thing," Ethan responded.

Ethan's grip on Astrid's shoulder tightened and his head lowered to blindly look at her above the top frame of his glasses. "One more thing, Astrid," he said. His left hand came up and he pointed one finger towards the student, just as a father giving instructions would do.

With a half joking, half serious face, Ethan said to Astrid, "I don't want to see you dropping out of school in the future because you have to take care of a baby."

They both smiled to one another and then Astrid happily skipped out of the room to go about her day.

Before the door could close behind the Indonesian student, it was swung back open. A fellow teacher made her way into Mr. Pleate's classroom. It was the 12th grade English teacher, Ms. Candice Vaughn.

Candice was a stunning, beautiful young woman. Even after the previous four years of studying in University of California, Los Angeles, she still looked the same as she did in high school. She had short, unnatural blonde hair that reached her shoulders. The natural dark brown was easily seen in the roots of her hair. She was tall, at about five feet, nine inches, and she was model-thin. She had high cheekbones which didn't need the light blush she routinely applied. Her lips were a lovely pink, not too thick and not too thin. They concealed a wonderful smile that pushed out a single dimple on her left cheek. But her most stunning features were her eyes. They had a very exotic look to them. They were slightly slanted, like an Asian person's, which gave her Caucasian background a nice mix. They were bold and she would use them to deeply express any feeling she had within her.

Ms. Vaughn's personality went along with her eyes. She was a straight-forward girl who spoke her mind. She would use her blunt words to get whatever she wanted. 'Fierce' could describe her.

She also had a crush on Ethan.

"Hey, handsome," she said to Ethan as he was dismounting the table in which he sat. "How was class?"

"It was good. Nothing out of the ordinary happened."

Ethan got a confused look on his face. "How did you get here so fast? You're on the other side of campus."

Candice replied with a grin, "My kids were 'good', so I let them go a little early."

Mr. Pleate let out a small laugh.

"So when are you going to let me fuck you?" Candice asked, with her grin still plastered on.

Ethan's eyebrows raised and a smile grew. He replied, "Come on, now, Candy. You know that will never happen."

Ethan's smile slowly got bigger and bigger, and his eyes got brighter and brighter. A short silence followed.

Candice's grin turned into a grimace.

"You're not still after that nerdy secretary chick, are you?" she asked with disappointment and partial disgust.

More silence coupled with Ethan's now ear-to-ear smile answered the question.

"Oh, my god!" Candice exclaimed. "What the hell do you see in her? With her big ass glasses, stringy hair and lack of fashion…"

Ethan clasped his hands over his chest, where his heart presumably lay beneath. He looked up and said, "I know! Isn't she great!?!"

Candice rolled her eyes and said to Ethan, shaking her head, "Dude, you're never going to get her away from her boyfriend. Nerd love is too strong and can't be broken."

"I'm on my way to see her now," Ethan started a light jog toward the exit of the classroom. "Wish me luck!"

Still facing the front of the class, Candice yelled back, "You're wasting your time! You should be fucking me!"

Ethan jogged to the main office building of the school. Before he opened the door to where the receptionists sat, he made sure he looked presentable. He jiggled the knot in his tie back and forth to feel for the correct position. He looked down at his shirt to ensure cleanliness. He took a deep breath, opened the door and made his way inside.

"Hello, ladies," Ethan said to the room with four females sitting behind desks. "You all look amazingly beautiful today. But Miss Sara looks exceptionally beautiful today!"

Ethan pulled up a chair and sat next to Sara Li.

Without raising her head from her paperwork, Sara smiled and said, "Oh, stop it, Ethan. I look exactly the same as yesterday and the day before."

"That's not true. Every day you become more and more gorgeous in my eyes. After we grow old together, you will have taken every ounce of beauty that this world has to offer."

"Stop it," Sara said again, still smiling. "You exaggerate too much."

"You deserve only the truth, my dear Sara," Ethan said.

Sara wasn't what the majority of guys in America would consider 'hot' or 'beautiful' or any synonym of those descriptions. She was a typical girl who had her roots in a small town of China. She had very light skin, long black hair stretching to the small of her back and dark eyes. She was thin, like most Chinese girls. She had a small nose that matched one a doll would wear and she had thin lips. She wore very little makeup and didn't really need to trim her eyebrows. She dressed similar to most girls in China – in a cute, schoolgirl kind of way. But no remarkable feature really stood out about her – except to Ethan.

Although she was a very average Chinese girl, she was very unique to Ethan for an obvious reason: she was Chinese. She was a *traditional* Chinese girl. That implies she was raised as a child to cherish certain aspects of life. She understood the value of work and money. She respected her family and would do anything for them. She grew up hearing snippets of Confucius' teachings and understood the meaning to countless Chinese proverbs. She was well-spoken and studied hard in school. And she always had high expectations for herself.

But above all, for Ethan, she very much *looked* Chinese.

I believe from a very young age, boys begin to grow particular tastes or attractions toward girls. Many men are attracted to women's breasts while other men would rather intrusively place their hands on round, firm buttocks. These interests don't go too far from these two particular body parts. Attractions towards other features like eyes, hair, personality or even feet, I think, are learned as the person grows and experiences and sees different types of these. Attraction to a particular race or ethnicity falls within these learned preferences. Some people learn to be attracted to Chinese, Hispanics, African American or whatever ethnicity they deem sexy. Ethan undoubtedly loved Asian women – in particular, Chinese, Korean or Japanese women.

"This is for you, my beautiful," Ethan said to Sara, holding out a hand containing a cut-out piece of paper with writing on it. "It's a poem I wrote for you from the bottom of my heart."

Ethan smiled at Sara.

Sara slowly reached for the gift. Her chin and eyebrows were puckered up, as if to say 'that is the sweetest thing anyone has ever done for me'.

"That is the sweetest thing anyone has ever done for me," she converted her facial expression into audible words.

"Go ahead and read it out loud," Ethan said to her.

Sara hesitantly looked down at the note and read aloud.

"'With every sunrise, I yearn to see the warmth you radiate. It relaxes me and breaks the long, cold night without you in my arms. The only thing I can do is wait, to wait for the happiest day of my life when you tell me 'I do''."

The other ladies in the room let out a harmonic, "Aww, that's so cute!"

Sara smiled, looked up to Mr. Pleate, and said, "That's so sweet of you, Ethan. Really. But you know as well as I know; I have a boyfriend."

"Yes, I know," Ethan said. "But you need to get rid of him so you can be with me. I'll treat you right. We'll live an awesome life together, in my studio apartment. After a long day's work, I'll massage your aches away and I'll cook us up some macaroni and cheese for dinner. The dinner may not be all that great but I do know how to whip up a tasty dessert." Ethan winked at Sara.

She gave a playful angry look at Ethan and gave him a slap on the arm.

"讨厌 (tao yan)!" she told him, which means 'I hate you' in Mandarin – but in a cute way.

"Get rid of him and come be with me and have my two baby girls I want in the future," Ethan continued to deliver. "But you better not give me a boy. Or else I'll leave you," he jokingly said with a fake serious look on his visage.

"I'm sorry, Ethan," Sara began to break his heart yet again. "There is nothing wrong with my boyfriend. He is a good guy. I can't break up with him. Thank you so much for all the sweet things you do for me, but I can't be yours."

Ethan's heart felt as if it were about to rupture. He foolishly thought that day would be the day Sara would stray away from her boyfriend and finally accept Ethan. But instead she dropkicked Ethan's heart yet again.

He slouched forward in his chair. He turned his head to the side, away from Sara, afraid he would burst into tears if he continued to look at her. His head slumped and his gaze focused on insignificant fibers on the carpeted floor. He felt as important to the world as that thread was at that moment. Ethan's throat swelled and blood started going to his face with minor embarrassment. He didn't want to be seen. He wanted to crawl under a desk and wait until every last soul had left the school campus until he would make his escape. One of his brows twitched down as if it were trying to hide the eye below. Maybe it thought if he couldn't see anything, then nothing could see him. His kind gesture didn't get the response he was hoping for.

Defeated and without saying another word, Ethan slowly got up and walked out of the office, while Sara was watching him with sympathetic eyes.

Even after the hundreds of times Sara had rejected him, Ethan still hurt deeply inside for each new occurrence of 'no, sorry Ethan'. It is devastating to know you can't be with the person you love. And indeed Ethan was in love with Sara.

Love. What is love? That's a difficult question. To some people, it could mean putting a partner's wants and needs before all others. Seeing that your lover is aching from a hard-working day and being there to massage away the tension that was built up can be satisfying to both parties. Cooking a lovely dinner to be served amidst a romantic setup with candles and soft music goes beyond fulfilling the basic need of nourishment. Having warm clothes set aside, waiting and ready to be used by your partner during the frosty months of the year would show a thoughtful and caring side to anyone. Buying the latest copy of your wife's favorite Cosmo magazine while shopping for cigarettes at the market keeps her wants in mind. Sacrificing your craving for vegetable lasagna and opting for that quiet little Mexican restaurant where the two of you first met adds a romantic touch to your partner's undying love for carne asada tacos.

The feeling of comfort and security is important to any relationship, especially for women, and some can define love as just this. Having the peace of mind to be able to tell your partner anything is unique and should be cherished. Knowing that exposing your fetish of being asphyxiated while having sex to your loving partner will be kept a secret between the two of you is a form of trust which goes beyond the bond you have with your best friend of 20 years. Having your lover there to support your thoughts, actions and decisions builds an amazing sense of emotional closeness to one another.

Emotional duality is strong enough to be love on its own. Emotion is one the most important things that separates humans from other animals. Being able to 'feel' happiness, sadness, loneliness, emptiness or joy is something most people take for granted. This gift is something we experience every day and allows us to be more than just zombies going about the routine of daily life. It is extraordinarily important because it allows us to empathize with others. Sharing a moment in one's life past its face-value with a partner can make the occasion euphorically rewarding. Friends become more than just friends when they learn how to share an emotion. The relationship deepens and strengthens. The connection between them becomes almost indestructible. True love is said to consist of this attachment.

As for Ethan, love is a feeling that is unexplainable to him. His stomach drops with nervousness every time he knows he is soon to meet Sara. The pores on his skin begin to open up to squeeze out beads of sweat. His mouth dries. He begins to speak a bit more rapidly. His mind becomes easily distracted. With all of this, he tries his best to stay focused. There is no other situation, person, occasion, fear, want or anything else that makes these things happen to him. These occurrences are unique to being around Sara Li and only Sara Li. And that is what love is to Ethan.

"Why don't you just give him a chance?" Rachel, a colleague of Sara, told her. "He does such sweet things for you."

"And he's so fine, too!" another receptionist, Amanda, said.

"Yeah, come on, girl," Tabetha, a heavy set, African American woman receptionist said. "Do you know how many girls want a piece of that? The entire female staff of teachers want to catch that for their own."

"Ya, he's the sweetest guy I've ever seen, Sara," Amanda added. "He would make the perfect boyfriend, surely."

"Girls, stop," Sara defended. "I really can't just throw my boyfriend John to the side. He's a good guy, too. It wouldn't be fair to him. You must understand that. Put yourself in John's shoes."

Then silence. The girls raised their eyebrows and all went back to the paperwork in front of them; except Sara only stared at the papers. She was preoccupied with contemplation.

'He *is* a really nice guy,' she thought to herself. 'He treats me nicely and does many sweet things for me. I wonder what it would be like to have an American boyfriend like Ethan. I wonder if my parents would even accept me seeing an American guy. And he really *is* handsome!'

A half smile formed on Sara's face as she dreamed of the hundreds of possibilities in a matter of seconds. Oddly enough, though, no negative thoughts about her and Ethan being together managed to squeeze their way into her daydream.

And who did Sara think she was fooling before when she said her current boyfriend John was a good guy? She knew as much as everyone else in the room that John didn't treat her with the fullest respect. I mean, he didn't beat her or lock her up in a cage or anything else as sadistic as that.

John Wang grew up in a traditional Chinese household. His parents were very happy to have a son on the first try. Ever since birth, John's parents did everything they could to ensure their son's success in the future. Basic learning supplies such as reading blocks, building logs, children's books and miniature science experiments were bought to give John a head start in his studies. The Chinese way of thinking is the level of university degree a student acquired was directly related to the level of success they would achieve outside of school. This may or may not be true in the United States, but university degrees are still the most common choice to make for 18 year old American students.

John's father, Bing, was a hard-working man. He deeply loved money and would do anything to get as much of it as possible – even if it meant working 14 hour days and not spending a lot of time in the comfort of his own earnings. Bing was a small business man. He owned 4 small shops in downtown Los Angeles which sold clothing manufactured in China and shipped directly to him. He didn't actually need to be at the stores during operation, but he thought it was necessary to do so and being there would boost sales. It goes without saying he put all of his sweat and energy into his work. And John followed this example.

It was implanted in John's mind to do the same as his father and to strive to get as much money as he could by working hard.

In China, it is usually the males who have all the prosperous opportunities when it comes to job positions, family roles and decisions or social issues. It is a culture which holds the X chromosome carriers up on a pedestal. Husbands and wives all over China wish to give birth to sons so they could do well in society and earn lots of money through the heavily weighted system. If their sons do well, then the parents should be well taken care of when they grow old. Chinese families are very close and it is not uncommon to see a 65 year old man taking care of his 90 year old mother in the same household.

But it is because of this special treatment towards males that China went through – and is still going through, in some parts – a terrible period in history. Due to China's overwhelming population, the government limited the amount of children a couple could have to only a single child.

So ever since the early 1980's when the provision was passed, if a Chinese couple could only have one child, they would rather it be a boy who could get all the wonderful benefits when he grew older. Abortions skyrocketed once expected mothers found out they were carrying a female. It got to a point when abortions were given by uncertified people using unsafe facilities and equipment. The current law forbidding aborting a child after the second trimester didn't stop desperate would-be mothers 20 years ago from performing the procedure in the seventh or eighth month of pregnancy.

With this recent history still spilling over into the present day, the Chinese still view females as slightly less than males. It is neither good nor bad. This cannot be judged as either good or bad. It is a culture issue. All cultures are different and should be respected in their own right.

But unfortunately, John upheld this mindset and carried it over to America. He always thought Sara Li was less than he. He would give more care and thought into his cellular phone instead of his own girlfriend.

'What if I start dating Ethan?' Sara thought. 'All of those wonderful things he does for me would be so great to experience as his girlfriend. It would be a huge change for the better.'

'Oh, my God! Do you hear what you are saying?!' Sara questioned her inner self. 'If you're saying it would be a change for the better, then that means you truly aren't happy with John! That means maybe you really want to be with Ethan! Oh, my! What should I do?!'

Sara Li was in a dilemma.

She contemplated in silence a bit more to herself, and then said out loud to no one in particular, "I'm going to make Ethan my boyfriend!"

Like a pack of feasting hyenas, the other girls of the office let out cheers and wails to give support to their sister.

"You go get him, girl!" Tabetha said.

"That a girl!" Rachel hollered.

Chapter Two

Driving through the residential streets of Pasadena, Jaime was on his way to make another delivery in his unmarked truck. He originally picked up this job to help out a cousin's new business, but he enjoyed the gig so much, he wanted to continue making deliveries even after the cousin's business was doing well enough to hire its own drivers.

The job was a piece of cake. I mean, really, how difficult is it to make an average of 10 deliveries in the course of six hours? It wasn't very. More than half of the workday was spent at lunch or on an arbitrary break to relieve 'stress', 'tension' or a calling of nature. The vans were equipped with custom sound systems so the employees could enjoy their favorite jams while stuck in traffic. The only thing Jaime needed to fret about was the hot southern California summers. But Jaime grew up with a father who turned the air conditioner on in his home only for special occasions. And Jaime's father, Miguel, didn't believe in special occasions.

But it wasn't the job itself that peaked Jaime's interest. It was the perks that came with the job. These perks weren't shown in writing anywhere. They weren't known during the 'interview process'. These perks needed to be learned and taken advantage of when the opportunity arose.

Jaime quickly found out about a big problem with most married couples: sex becomes void after the promise of loyalty is sealed. And later, hatred and resentment towards one another develops. There are countless wives out there who are in almost desperate need for sex and who have grown angry at their husbands for various issues – the most common being the husband is rarely home and is always 'too tired' to be intimate with their wives. Many women start giving away not only their partners' possessions, but themselves as well. All they really need is a reason to do so, which is where the 'delivery guy' comes into play. If worded correctly, a conversation could end up with tipping the delivery man with a set of golf clubs, an autographed baseball or with sex. Today's delivery from Jaime would end up with some sex.

The blaring of the old Dr. Dre song "Bang Bang" easily filled the quiet street of Ford Road. Jaime, with his delivery truck, slowed to a speed of about 20 miles per hour so the target house wouldn't be missed. Jaime squinted his eyes up the long driveways full of Mercedes Benz's and Porches to read out the numbers printed on the two story miniature mansions.

"...353...359...365," Jaime quietly said to himself.

The day was rather warm for April in the outskirts of Los Angeles. The thermometer which hung from the rear view mirror read 90 degrees. It felt worse driving through that area of Pasadena – a residential street with no trees to shade the ground below. Sweat was beading on Jaime's forehead and had already formed patches under the short sleeves of his button up, collared, white work shirt that was too wide for Jaime's slim figure.   His undershirt was already darkened on the neckline from moisture. All of this gave

Jaime a good reason to invite himself into another person's home to cool off with a glass of water.

Jaime slowed his truck to a stop in front of 15369 Ford Road. He never parked in a customer's driveway; the massive delivery truck was too hard to maneuver while backing up.

"Here we are," Jaime said to himself.

He grabbed a small box, about the size of a novel, from the dashboard. Even though he had lost multiple packages from banking turns too sharply, he still thought it was more convenient to have small boxes ready to go, waiting up on the dash. After all, some packages just get 'lost in the mail'.

Jaime hopped out of the tall driver's seat, box in hand. He was relieved to get out of the kiln he was in. He started a flamboyant, slow jog up the driveway to the doorstep of the immaculate, Romanesque temple. He wanted to get as much air to his sweaty pores as possible, to cool them off. And after one last skip onto a raggedy doormat that did not belong in that part of the city, Jaime rang the doorbell – or rather pushed a button to set off multiple sized gongs within the house.

As he waited for the owner to approach the door, Jaime kept himself entertained by banging his head up and down to the beat of Dr. Dre's hit that was echoing in his mind. The wait lasted about 30 seconds, and it was well worth it.

Who better to show up behind the door to a temple than a goddess. Her skin was tanned and sparkling as if millions of stars were contained within her. She stood at about five feet, six inches tall and had a slim body. Calling her busty would be an understatement while she wore a sexy collared businesswoman blouse with the buttons undone down to the bridge of her lacy, golden threaded black bra which pushed her breasts to the tipping point of being exposed. The red top flared out slightly, just past her waist, giving way to a skirt which was no longer than four inches past the extent of her vagina. It looked like she wore stockings, but the mirage was from the glistening of the lotion she used on those parts of her body. Her feet nestled in smart, black high heels. Why was she all dressed up as if she were the CEO of a Fortune 500 company?

The goddess was 29 years old and very much looked her age. She didn't carry herself like an immature college girl, but rather like she controlled everything around her. She had big, bold, dark eyes that came to a point on the side of her temples. Her eyes were dressed with long, thick eyelashes. She could easily speak her mind with just her gaze. Her nose went high up, with a narrow bridge going down and almost too far out. It went well with her slender face. Her nostrils were more oval than round which gave way to a hairless moustache region that was void of outlining wrinkles. She had thin lips, but they were very defined and protruded out to a beautiful length. Sparkles continued inside her mouth from tri-annual whitening at her dentist's office. Her hair was partially bunned with the ends bursting outward like the tail feathers of a peacock. A long group of hair swung down across her forehead to wrap around her left ear.

"Hi, there," Jaime broke his gawk. "You must be the lovely Mrs. Stergent."

Jaime had gotten the information from the shipping label on the package.

"Why, yes. Yes, I am," she replied in a soft, sensual voice. "But I want you to call me 'Nay'."

"That's an interesting name," Jaime said with a questionable face.

"No, it's just short for Naomi."

"That makes a whole lotta sense. This heat's got my mind swimmin'."

"It *is* quite warm out there today. You should come in and rest for a while," Naomi said, a smile starting to come through. "You can have a glass of water, juice or maybe a glass of champagne?"

"I'm sorry, but I only drink champagne during a time of celebration."

As a matter of fact, Jaime had never drunk champagne before. He wasn't big on drinks that would normally be found in the hands of women. His elixirs of choice were beer, vodka or tequila.

"Well, then let's make this a celebration," Naomi told Jaime, with a naughty grin replacing her smile.

Jaime walked into the temple of Naomi, accepting her suggestion. The house was very modern on the inside. The color scheme was a very clean white and red. Lounge sofas and chairs were about and charcoal gray, thin but tall art formations decorated once-empty areas. Walkways were tiled with dark gray flooring and common areas were carpeted in white. The walls had no decorations; they were plainly left white. The downstairs had a vast kitchen with two islands, two living areas, a large dining area and a full bar loaded with top shelf booze.

"Just take a seat on the sofa, there." Naomi signaled which sofa by nodding her head in the proper direction. "I'll take care of everything. You just rest for a bit."

Jaime liked where this was going. It looked as if the roles were going to be switched, with him being pampered. So he did as he was told and made himself cozy into the comfortable sofa and relaxed in a slouched position. He continued to look around and examined the place, still awestruck.

"I'm actually really glad you stopped by," Naomi said from the bar. "There is something I need you to help me with…"

"Sure. Do you need me to move some furniture or kill a spider or something like that?" Jaime jokingly said.

"Not quite, sweetie."

Nay walked back to the living room in which Jaime awaited, now holding two glasses of bubbly champagne. She sat right next to Jaime and placed the glasses on a clear crystal table in front of them. She turned her body towards his and put one arm around Jaime's neck. And with the other arm, she reached for his chest and smoothly ran her hand over it.

In a sexier voice, she said, "I've been needing something for a very long time now… My loser husband doesn't fuck me anymore."

Her tone quickly went from sweet to harsh and full of hatred when she said, "That bastard's probably sleeping with another bitch…"

Jaime ignored the hypocrisy and just sat back and listened.

The sexy voice returned. "Do you think you can help me out?" Naomi asked with puckered lips.

'Fuck yeah I'll fuckin' fuck you!' Jaime thought in his mind. But he answered Naomi's question by throwing his tongue in her mouth.

Amazing. That was the only thing that was stamped in Jaime's brain as he climbed back into his truck an hour and a half later. A big smile was plastered on his face. He was in heaven – still. Jaime had seen a lot of sex in his life, but what he had just experienced was something that was unknown to him up to that point. It was complete nirvana at times. It was a breathless cry for help at times. It was absolute animalistic fornication at times. It was an understanding of the true meaning of life at times. It was obtaining the knowledge of decoding the female orgasm with the excitement to be able to reveal the information to humanity for the first time ever. It was 'amazing'.

Jaime sat in the driver's seat, speechless. He stared out forward through the windshield. His eyes were glazed over, nothing caught their attention. He felt relieved but tired at the same time.

A short while had silently elapsed when Jaime's meditative state was broken by the vibration of his mobile phone. Shaking off his numbed concentration, he reached over and opened the glove box that housed his phone during work hours. He opened the latch and took out the vibrating device. He looked down to see the name of the caller: 'steph'.

Stephanie Guzman was Jaime's girlfriend since the two were high school seniors four years ago. They had been through some good times and bad times, just like any other relationship. But in this one, the bad times were usually caused by Jaime's cheating. That was the biggest basis of problems for Stephanie and Jaime.

Jaime was a very good looking guy. His two Hispanic parents gave birth to a tanned skinned, light brown haired, hazel eyed boy with chiseled features. From far, Jaime had an average body, referencing his height and weight. But up close, one would notice that his defined facial structure, his cheek bones, eyebrow line and chin were all well-formed. He had a long face and a full head of short, wavy hair. His eyes were big and bold and his teeth were brilliant and straight. It only took about a week at the gym to cut Jaime's muscles out from hiding. They weren't overly done, just enough to fill any Street Fighter role in Hollywood. A person would have to look with extreme detail to find an imperfection. But the thing that most girls found irresistible about Jaime was his smile and character.

Jaime was optimistic about everything. Even during his 'lowest' moments, he still carried a smile and probably even laughed. He was fun to hang out with because he never took things too seriously. He fully believed in enjoying life and he certainly had done that. He was always joyous and happy, yet was laid back and simple. He learned to enjoy life itself rather than physical objects, since his low income family didn't have enough money to spare for extras.

It was this which made many beautiful girls flock to Jaime's side. He always had girls flirting with him. He would literally have the most gorgeous girls around trying to spark up conversations just so he would consider getting to know them. And yet Jaime was still able to keep his cool and talk smoothly to them all. And he did just that. He never neglected anyone.

Needless to say, Jaime had lots of opportunities to covet any man's dream girl. And he followed up on most of these opportunities, just like most other guys would do.

Jaime cheated on Stephanie numerous times in the four years together. Stephanie knew about most of the deeds, too. But she always forgave Jaime and took him back. Her friends thought the reason for taking him back was because she was a practicing Catholic and believed in forgiveness. Others thought it was because it was her first love. Both of these reasons were half true, but only Stephanie knew the real answer for taking Jaime back after he slept with another girl. The real reason could have been the way Jaime made her feel. He treated her perfectly when they were together. Or maybe it was because she was already accidentally impregnated twice by him. Even though her actions are not uncommon, only she can reveal the actual reason for giving a cheat another chance, time and time again.

Jaime answered the phone, "Hi, baby. What's up?"

"Hi, babe. What are you doing?" Stephanie asked.

"I just finished dropping off a package at this huge mansion out here in Pasadena," Jaime explained. "Steph, you should see the houses out here. They're so tight and crazy big. One of these houses could fit like 16 Mexican families."

"You should buy us a house out there, then, babe," Stephanie told Jaime.

"Haha. Yeah, right. Not with the beans and rice I get paid in."

"Well, at least we know we won't starve…" Stephanie finished the joke.

"Listen, babe," Stephanie continued with the reason she called. "Let's get together tonight for dinner, ok?"

"Yeah, sure thing. I get off work at six. How about we meet at Spaghetti Heaven at like 6:30?" Jaime asked.

"Ok, babe. I'll see you there. And don't be late!"

"I won't, baby girl. See you then."

Jaime had another four hours to finish up two deliveries before meeting his other half. And as he looked at the addresses of the remaining two packages, he realized he would have lots of time to fool around.

He started up the engine and began to drive out of wonderland, in the direction of Johnny's Burgers he had passed before to quench his other appetite.

Chapter Three

As soon as Sara stepped out of her office after finishing her paperwork for her job at the high school, she excitedly took out her cellular phone from her Doraemon purse and began to type out a text message.

'Let's meet up tonight for dinner. I have to talk to you about something,' she spelled out.

Then she stood in the parking lot where her car was sitting. She froze and stared down at what she had written. She was a bit in shock knowing she was going to go through with this initial message to try to start a relationship with Ethan Pleate. Or maybe she wasn't ready. This was very unlike her usual self. She never did anything as drastic as this. Her decisions were normally backed by weeks of planning and examining all different possible repercussions to her actions. But there she was. Standing on the heated black pavement of a Chino Hills high school, all alone to make the decision to send the signal from her heart to her brain to lower her right thumb to cover the lozenge shape on her phone marked with 'send', then to lift the finger, to reach the point of no return. To go to a feeling she had never experienced before. To begin the stressful and sweaty waiting time she would have to go through to receive a response from the person who could possibly turn out to be her husband in the future. The man who could possibly be the one to help her have the son and daughter she wanted before she reached the age of 28. The man who could be there to hold her at night and keep her safe during times of uncertainty. The man who could eat her delicious cooking for the rest of their lives.

Or, he could be the man to shatter all these thoughts and disintegrate any feelings they had between one another. But she didn't want to think of that possibility.

Chapter Four

Astrid walked out to the front of her high school to meet her boyfriend where he did every other day – at the flagpole. She kept thinking of what Mr. Pleate had told her earlier. She definitely was uneasy about the thought of sex. It was more of a fear of the unknown. She was still a virgin and had not even done anything sexual beyond making out with her tongue. She was still a very innocent girl. Sex was never openly talked about in her family nor did her parents even show the slightest physical affection toward one another while Astrid was present. The only 'experiences' she had were the stories her friends would talk about in their groups.

'I'm obviously not ready for sex if I'm shaking like a Chihuahua in 80 degree weather,' she told herself.

She sat on the cement base of the flagpole once she had arrived. But she didn't need to wait long for her boyfriend Ronnie to come tapping on her shoulder.

"Hey, beautiful girl," he greeted Astrid.

"Hi, baby," she replied, tilting her head back to see Ronnie. She shot up like a spring and gave Ronnie a quick kiss and a big hug.

"Wow, baby, did you lift weights all day today?" Ronnie jokingly asked Astrid. "Your bear hug has gotten way stronger."

Astrid giggled, "Hehe, no. I just missed you, is all."

Ronnie didn't even need to put his arms around Astrid; she was doing all the work with her tight squeeze.

A moment later, Astrid let go of her human trap.

"So what's the plan for today, baby?" Ronnie asked. "Do you gotta be home right now or do you wanna come over to my house to relax?"

"We can go to your place," Astrid responded. "My parents won't be home until later on tonight."

Astrid took a second to revel in Ronnie's aura. She loved him deeply. She loved that he was able to show her exactly what love was. She cared a lot about Ronnie and only wished him the best.

When Astrid found out a bearing from Ronnie's skateboard had broke, she surprised her boyfriend by rushing over to the skate shop two blocks down and bought him the needed replacement. When Astrid learned Ronnie wasn't feeling well, she fixed him up a delicious bowl of homemade chicken noodle soup to personally deliver to his home. When Astrid saw her boyfriend doing poorly in a subject at school, she genuinely helped him study to get a better grade. And when Ronnie was not by Astrid's side, she truly missed him.

Astrid stood slightly back from Ronnie to check out his appearance. She loved his gorgeous, long, dirty blond hair that went down to his chin. His faded blue eyes made Astrid's insides melt. Long eyelashes stood at attention under unusually thin eyebrows. Ronnie had a large, high nose, but that didn't bother Astrid one bit. He had dazzling white teeth under a lazy smile unique to him. To Astrid, Ronnie had the body of a surfer boy.

"What the hell are you staring at me like that for?" Ronnie questioned Astrid, showing her his smile.

"No reason."

Astrid smiled back at Ronnie then quickly took his hand and said, "Come on. Let's go."

They began to walk down the street in the direction of Ronnie's house.

"So how's your day, baby?" Astrid asked Ronnie.

"It was good. My buddy told me a trick to fool the machine that checks scan-tron test papers," Ronnie began to explain. "He said to just smear a thin coat of lip balm all over the scan-tron paper and that'll mess up the machine to give you a perfect score."

Ronnie briefly paused, then said, "I don't know if it'll work or not, but I guess it's worth a try."

"Baby, don't try to cheat the system. You know I'll help you if you're struggling in any subject. Just ask me to study with you."

"Hmm, maybe you're right. I need to try failing more classes so I can have you over my house more nights," Ronnie said with a grimace.

"Don't be silly. You don't need to *try* to fail your classes."

Ronnie gave Astrid a love tap on the back of her head.

"Today, my friend Ashley told me that she's gonna try to break your friend Alex up with his girlfriend," Astrid said.

"What?! Haha! What for?"

"She wants a piece of that. She thinks he's cute."

"Haha, well, let her try. Catherine gives Alex everything he needs. There's no way he's gonna leave her."

"I dunno... Ashley can be a real manipulative bitch. She usually gets anything or anyone she wants."

"We'll see if she's got what it takes."

Ronnie looked up to the sky to see a small plane buzz through the pale clouds above. He squinted his eyes and subconsciously squeezed Astrid's hand tighter. Astrid looked over to Ronnie and smiled. She didn't need to hear the words come out of her boyfriend's mouth to know he wanted to pilot people around the world in his future. Every time a plane or even a beautiful bird flew above, he would pause and gawk. Every time his family would fly to a vacation spot, he wouldn't get any sleep the night before because of his anticipation.

"Some day, baby," Astrid told Ronnie. "You'll be up there soon enough."

"Yeah. All's I gotta do is wish upon a star..."

"Don't sweat it, Ronnie. I'll do whatever it takes to help you get your pilot's license."

Ronnie looked over to Astrid and gave a loving smile.

"So what do you wanna do this weekend, love?" Astrid asked.

"I'm not sure yet. I think a few of us might head over to Childress Park to skate for a bit tomorrow. Do you wanna come with?"

"It's fuckin' hot outside, babe. You guys are crazy. I sweat my ass off just watching you guys and there you are doin' flips and twirls and somersaults."

"Hey, hey! I'm not forcing you to go, now," Ronnie said, laughing.

"Alright. Go with me to buy one of those big sombrero hats first. Then we can go together after that."

"Okay, but not until like one or two in the afternoon... I need to get my sleep. I love sleep more than anything."

"Even more than me?" Astrid questioned as she rocked her head back and forth.

"You're my mistress to sleep."

Astrid rolled her eyes at Ronnie.

"Come on," Ronnie said. "It works out so perfectly. The both of you don't mind if I see the other."

"Yeah, we'll see who's there for you in the end."

"Well, if I die in my sleep the way I want to, then I guess we both know the answer to your little riddle."

"How much do you love me?" Astrid asked under an exaggerated smile.

"About as much as I love pissin' blood after I fall from my skateboard," Ronnie quickly responded.

"Whatever, punk!" Astrid said, laughing.

They had reached a small plaza filled with different kinds of stores and shops, including a barber shop, a pizzeria, a car wash and even an Army recruiting center. On the sidewalk beside the street leading to the shopping center, there was a man doing sign spinning to advertise the mom and pop's pizza joint within the shopping center.

Sign spinning is a form of marketing used to attract customers who are driving by. A worker would hold a plastic sign, usually painted in flashy colors and shaped like a large arrow, guiding passersby to the target location. Sometimes these sign spinners would get fancy and learn to spin and flip the signs in elaborate ways, either to attract more attention or to simply beat the boredom. Over the past few years, sign spinners have gotten quite imaginative, with even their own body doing flips over the plastic arrow or tossing the sign meters into the air to be caught in a way that was made to look easy, despite its difficulty.

But this guy standing on the sidewalk of Pipeline Avenue was rather lame. He didn't try any of the tricky moves. One would think he would have learned a small routine in all the years he had spent there. Five years so far, to be exact. The man was in his early 20's and he had already spent over five years as a sign spinner. All the local citizens of the city knew who he was. The young man stood out there four days a week for the past five years in the same spot holding the same sign on one of the busiest streets of the city. Not many knew his name, but many Chino Hills residents would be able to notice him in a crowd of people with his strawberry hair and matching long sideburns.

"Check that guy out, babe," Ronnie said to Astrid, nodding in the direction of the sign holder. "How long do you think he's going to be doing that for?"

"He's been doing that same thing for as long as I can remember," Astrid disappointedly replied. "He'll probably be doing something like that for the rest of his life."

"Yeah. But who knows… Maybe he's just doing that while he gets a degree in college in rocket science or something. Maybe one day he'll be the one to develop a new form of propulsion for our rocket systems so we can travel to the farthest reaches of space in the near future."

"Ugh, knock off the science talk. You're starting to sound like my physics teacher."

"Haha. But you never know. You can't judge people just by lookin' at 'em."

"Hey! You're the one who brought it up!" Astrid defended herself.

"I was merely asking a simple question. You're the one with a black heart saying he's going to be a low-life for the rest of his days."

"You put those words in my mouth!"

"I did not!" Ronnie said laughing. "Don't blame your cruelty and hatred toward others on me!"

"I hate you today!" Astrid said with a fake angry look.

"I hate you every other day!" Ronnie retaliated.

This was the kind of humor that always surrounded the couple. They loved to tell one another just how little they loved each other and to create false cheating stories just to irritate one another. It was all fun and games. Neither of them really meant those hateful words.

"Awww, I could really go for some Court Jester's tacos right now!" Ronnie said as they approached another shopping area with many fast food restaurants.

"Those tacos are disgusting! They aren't even real tacos!"

"But they're so damn good!"

"Yeah, you know that 'meat' that's in those tacos?" Astrid rhetorically asked. "That's not even real meat! My friend once told me that she went there before and told the people that worked there that she was vegetarian. She asked them if they had anything without meat. Guess what they said."

"Try yo momma's food?" Ronnie smartly asked.

"Psh, my mom's food is the best and you know it."

"Whatever! It's all the same to me. It's always rice and some weird mix of different kinds of mutant vegetables I've never seen before smothered with gooey sauces that sting every inch of my stomach."

"Mmmm, I could go for some of *that* right now!"

"I hope you didn't inherit your mom's cooking skills," Ronnie stabbed at Astrid. "I'm gonna want meat 'n potatoes for dinner just like every other man in America!"

"You jerk! I'm gonna make you go eat Court Jester's every day in the future."

"Ahhh, that'll be heaven!" Ronnie was beginning to drool.

After crossing the busy intersection adjacent to the restaurant center, Astrid and Ronnie reached the backyard of Ronnie's house, which faced the busy, loud engines of passing motorists. The six foot high brick wall that separated the street with Ronnie's parents' backyard worked amazingly well at keeping the noise where it belonged.

"Come on, babe. Leg up," Ronnie told Astrid as he squatted down on one knee and held out his clasped hands, ready to give Astrid a boost over the wall.

"Oh, for a minute there I thought you were going to propose to me."

"Sorry, love. I already asked your friend Heather and she said 'yeah'."

"Shut up and get me over this damn wall."

"As a mat' fact, she's having my baby. Twins, actually. And she wanted me to promise not to name one of them Astrid if they turn out to be girls. She really hates that name."

"I'm gonna punch you in the jugular if you keep it up," Astrid's less feminine side began to show itself.

Astrid carefully hopped down from the top of the wall after being lifted up. She landed on a pile of dirt in the corner of the yard where Ronnie's mother, Elizabeth, had been planning to nurse an orange tree. She never got around to it.

Ronnie slammed down onto the dirt, leaving a compressed imprint of the bottoms of his skate shoes in the soft dirt.

They both walked over to a bench swing that was only used by the two of them. Astrid was a split second faster than Ronnie so she got the prime position of lying down. But then again, Ronnie had no problem lying on top of her, cupping his hands on both sides of her face. He looked deep into her eyes, thinking how much he enjoyed being with her.

He never had a dull moment with her. They rarely argued – aside from the playful arguments. All of his cares and fears and worries went out the door when he was beside Astrid. She made him feel 'free'.

An unbelievable sense of freedom can come from not needing to accomplish a thing, from having no concern that needed to be dealt with. When you throw all your thoughts pertaining to errands or homework or payments or appointments off to the side and live for the moment, you can get a sense of unconditional 'freedom'. Just think of a time in your past when you had a week vacation at that beachside resort. The beautiful white sand beach going along sparkling, warm blue water was great and all, but it really didn't hold a candle to the feeling you got from not having to do anything for an entire seven days. When the only worry you are concerned about is waking up in time to catch the breathtaking and astonishing sunset, then you are in good shape.

Ronnie smiled as his stare pierced hers. They were both feeling the same emotion. They were both linked together as one, sharing the same love for one another. Time froze. The birds and soft sounds of car engines faded to non-existence. A black hole of emptiness surrounded the two, leaving no distractions to go between them. Except for the heat. It was still damn hot.

Seconds of staring turned into minutes until Ronnie moved in to give Astrid a long, wet kiss. They wrapped their lips around one another's and exchanged tongues. There was no awkwardness to it; they both were great kissers. Their tongues kept loose and flexible and didn't get into anything's way. Their heads didn't jerk in any direction. Instead, they effortlessly rocked back and forth at appropriate intervals. Their hands didn't lie to their sides like those of a stiff corpse. Rather they were utilized to enhance pleasure by squeezing and caressing the more sensitive parts of the body. Both Ronnie and Astrid melted together as one.

About three minutes passed with saliva build up becoming overwhelming at times. Then Ronnie, almost instinctively, placed his left hand over Astrid's pelvic area, where her vagina was hiding underneath her tight jeans. He began to smoothly rub, back and forth, in an attempt to get her juices flowing. It made Astrid a tad uncomfortable, and she pressed her buttocks deep into the bench, to soften Ronnie's touch. Astrid was now distracted and it affected her kissing. She froze her lips temporarily, every so often. The change was obvious to Ronnie.

"What's wrong, baby?" Ronnie asked Astrid, pushing his head up.

"I don't know, baby," she shyly responded. "I don't think I'm ready to do what you want me to do," her voice cracked.

"Come one, baby. There's nothing to be afraid of. I'll go slow and soft."

It wasn't Ronnie's first time with a girl. Ronnie had lost his virginity when he was in junior high school, at the age of 14. His first experience was only slightly awkward, compared to most told stories. He was a natural when it came to making a girl feel good in bed. From the get-go, he knew to put all focus and concentration into making his companion feel like a queen. For each of the six girls after the first he slept with, his sensual and caring style became better and more fulfilling. Whenever time permitted, Ronnie was able to give his partner multiple orgasms. He knew if he had done so, the girls would go crawling back to him for more and word would spread to up his chances at having more opportunities with more beautiful girls. He wanted it to seem like he was providing a service to these girls and they would be lucky if he accepted them and took them in to free them of their stress. Sex can be a powerful weapon.

"I don't know... I'm really scared," Astrid said with concern.

"Baby, we both love each other. This will just express the way we feel about one another in a physical way."

"Baby, I just don't think I can do it."

"Love, we've been goin' out for over six months..."

"There shouldn't be a time limit to having sex with someone."

"Alright, then. Whatever," Ronnie's tone of voice turned from sweet and loving to menacing and angered. He shot up from Astrid with a disappointed look on his face. "I'm gonna go to Josh's house. You can do whatever the hell you want."

Ronnie began to walk to the side of the backyard, towards the front of the house where the gate was.

"Ronnie, wait!" Astrid cried out.

But he didn't. He kept going. He reached to unlatch the door, walked through, and then was gone.

Not knowing how to feel or what to think, Astrid lay on the bench swing for 20 minutes before leaving for her own home, in tears.

Chapter Five

Jaime looked down at his watch to check his schedule. He wanted to ensure he would arrive on time for his dinner date with his girlfriend Stephanie. The two of them didn't get to spend much time together ever since Stephanie began her job at a small hair salon. She would work the reception when customers were present, and she would get informally taught how to cut hair correctly from one of the staff members when business was slow. She had high hopes to soon do the real thing one day to make a decent earning from salary and tips. And as for her stylist certification which would hang at her cutting station? Well, any document can be forged as long as you know someone who has the supplies and the lack of moral fiber.

'Hmm, let's see… five o'clock now…' Jaime formulated in his mind. 'I'll go ahead and drop this off real quick, head back to drop off the van, then should get to Spaghetti Heaven just on time.'

He had already pulled to the side of the residential street in Garden Grove where his final drop off would be. It was a much different neighborhood from the earlier one in Pasadena. This one was more 'real'. There were children playing in the street with toy guns and others tossing a football back and forth. Thick tree trunks sprawled way up in front of almost every moderately sized home. The branches which carried fresh green leaves sprouted over the lane, giving pockets of shade here and there. Cars from the past five decades were either being driven through, parked, or being slowly repaired or rotted away on front driveways. There were no massive eight-seater SUV's. There were no gaudy sports cars. There was only modest Americana. Parents were seen outside talking on their phones or chatting with other parents. Dogs roamed freely, birds chirped along.

Jaime reached down and picked up the package that was on the floor of the van between the driver's seat and the passenger's seat. He jumped out of the truck and was immediately greeted by a playful young boy.

"Hi, mister. What'cha got in the box?"

"Hey, buddy," Jaime replied. "Actually, I don't know what's in here. I'm just here to deliver this to whoever lives at this house."

"That's neat, mister. So you're like Santa Claus. Except you're really thin."

"That's right. So you better be good because I'll be watching you at night."

Jaime quickly turned his head and stood with his eyes cocked all the way to the side and his eyebrows lowered in confusion as he realized what he had just said wasn't something that should be said to a young boy.

The boy shook it off, didn't say another word and went on his way.

Jaime walked up the driveway to his target's location. He noticed a pink jump rope strewn about on the front lawn and a soccer ball to accompany it. He reached the heavy wooden door and gave it three firm knocks.

Not a moment later did a beautiful woman with the biggest natural breasts Jaime had ever seen on such a small frame swing the door open. Jaime swallowed his saliva incorrectly and gave chocking coughs while he looked at the balloons under the woman's strapless top.

"Oh, my! Are you okay?" the woman asked with concern as she reached to Jaime's back and gave it a few taps to calm the coughing.

Clearing his throat, Jaime replied in a stutter, "Yeah, yeah, yeah, sorry. I just have never seen such a beautiful woman before."

The woman smiled. "But all you did was look at my tits. How can you say I'm so beautiful and all if you only look at my tits?"

"Don't worry, babe," Jaime smoothly said. "I got the rest of you in my peripherals." Jaime pointed to his eyes with all ten of his fingers.

"Do you wanna see 'em?" she asked curiously with one eyebrow raised.

"Do I wanna see what?" Jaime asked, confused.

"My tits, silly. Do you wanna see my tits?"

Jaime gave a brief shocked expression, then replied, "My father always taught me: 'when a woman offers to show you her tits, you better goddamn accept!'"

She laughed. She then proceeded to lower the strapless top without hesitation. She didn't care she was in public. She didn't care if others saw. She was a sexy woman and didn't mind if others knew it. She released the beasts.

Jaime stood and stared. His saliva glands lost control. He ogled at the perfect breasts on the woman who was no taller than five feet. The areolas were larger than normal, but what Jaime loved was how far out the actual nipple protruded. They came out at least three quarters of an inch. Jaime also loved how they were already ready, standing at attention.

About 30 seconds passed.

"So are you just gonna stand there or are you gonna put one of these babies in your mouth?" the woman asked – or rather, demanded.

Jaime went at her like a zombie about to suck out Albert Einstein's brain. He pushed her deeper into her house and closed the door behind him with his right leg. And just like a hungry newly born baby, he engulfed the woman's massive breasts and swashed his tongue around to play with the nipples. Jaime's left hand let loose of the package it carried, for it was no longer a concern. They both ran into an ottoman sitting in the living room and the girl's knees buckled. She sat down and he sat on top of her, mouth still on tit. Then for some strange reason, Jaime remembered the jump rope and soccer ball in the front yard.

"Wait a minute!" Jaime said aloud. "Where are your kids?"

"Don't worry. They're down the street playing. They have never come home before dinner was ready."

"Oh, ok..."

Jaime continued to suck and lick.

"Wait a minute!" Jaime said aloud. "What about your husband?"

"Don't worry about him. He's just in the kitchen sharpening some knives."

Jaime jumped up like a spring releasing its energy. "What the fuck?!"

"Goddamn, boy. Settle down," she tried to ease Jaime. "I'm just kidding. He's at work. Don't fret."

Jaime continued where he left off.

Some people look down upon having sex with someone without being married to that person or even just having sex before you are married yourself. In recent times, many groups have come around the world teaching and practicing abstinence until marriage. And it's not just a religious idea. This way of thinking has made itself widely known in many cultures around the world, but religion is the main backer of this thought. Fundamental teachings of religions, including the major ones, teach to not give one's body out to just anyone. But where does this even come from and why now?

In ancient Greece, before the time of Christ, sexuality was much more a part of everyday life compared to today. We have unearthed pottery and documents depicting people walking either naked or just barely covering the genitals during normal day activity. And on many of these artifacts, there are paintings and/or descriptions of men and women engaging in sex. Sexual positions would be shown, maybe as a learning tool or maybe as an artist's preferred choice. Dildos and other sex toys were very common and often given as gifts in ancient Greece. The people were very open towards sex and a married man who slept with a slave wouldn't even be considered an adulterer. And the Romans weren't too far off from the Greeks, especially during the infamous reign of Caligula, or Julius Caesar.

And even further back, in ancient Egypt, clothing was even more revealing than that of today. Women usually wore a see-through gown only, while men would drape a cloth to cover his member. Egyptologists and archaeologists are recently uncovering new evidence of just how open the ancient Egyptians were. A new unveiling of a cave in the Valley of the Kings show entire walls filled with drawings of men and women having sex. Like the Greeks, the pictures show various positions a couple could try during copulation. Even the famous Queen Cleopatra was known to have a large share of sexual partners.

This day in age, most of us are familiar with the book Kama Sutra, at least by name and reputation. Ancient people in the subcontinent of India were one of the most sexual in all of human history. Sex was portrayed in literature, in pottery and also all over entire temples. The Khajuraho Temple in India is famous for its erotic carvings throughout the temple.

But we needn't look so far into the past to see a more open society. There are numerous cultures around the world today that are much more accepting of the idea of nudity and sex. The Discovery Channel has many examples of peoples who bear all or have sexual celebrations or rituals or even just practice polygamy.

So why have we become so closed off and so scared to discuss sex? Why has it become such taboo? It is human nature to have sex and reproduce. Human population has reached the seven billion mark so we obviously have lots of sex. If anything, we have more sex today, seeing that population growth has only recently skyrocketed. Why has such a natural activity become so uneasy to openly talk about? Where does the bad stigma come from? Who or what was the beginning of the new paradigm? I understand current times have given rise to new and deadly diseases that are transmitted via sexual activity, but these infections aren't spread solely because of the act. They are spread because of neglect for safety.

Chapter Six

Ethan stepped down from bus number 117, just like a child would, and began his short walk to his apartment two blocks away. It was only him and one other elderly lady who rode the bus that afternoon. Riding the bus was rather unconventional in a city – or region, even – where just about everyone drove a car. Sixteen year old high schoolers would get gifts of brand new trucks or small imported cars for their birthdays. But here was a man in his mid 20's riding the bus from place to place.

Ethan Pleate wasn't a poor man, but instead a very simple man. He didn't care for many luxuries in life, like having a big house, fancy car, high-end clothing or watches, or even expensive meals. He made enough money to have each one of these examples in his life, but he opted not to. He didn't value those things. In his eyes, there were things that were more important, more valuable, that he would try to attain. Ethan's Ferrari was a job which he truly enjoyed. His Rolex watch was discovering new music he could relate to. His massive house by the beach was finding and keeping true love. He accomplished the first part of his dream, but he hasn't completely closed the deal quite yet, so to speak.

Ethan had fallen in love before Sara. His longest relationship of two years taught him what love really was. That relationship opened his eyes and mind to what every person should strive for in their lives. He had many relationships and girlfriends before and after that one, but they were usually very short and loveless. His two year relationship taught him what the most important thing in the world was. It taught him how to live a 'complete' life. It taught him how sad, depressed, lonely and unfortunate a person is who didn't have a partner to love and be loved by. Having someone to intimately hold and caress at night can only be described as having complete emotional union. Having someone sitting across the table from you to joke about the latest gossip while having lunch at McDonald's is far better than sitting alone with your iPod and headphones, no matter how great the song is you are listening to. Seeing the words 'I love you and I can't wait to see you' come across your phone in a text message brings warmth to your heart. Just having the thought of that person you love go through your mind can have enough power to brighten the lowest of days. Having these things in your life makes it worth every second. To attain love is to attain happiness unknown to those who have never felt love.

When Ethan was not at work or with friends or family, which was a large portion of his life, he was very much alone. He felt an emptiness inside of him that pierced through to his soul. A void surrounded his being and would sometimes show itself with a blank expression on his face. Any passerby would know the problem Ethan had just by feeling his aura which was deeply missing a pertinent piece. Ethan knew this, but there wasn't much he could do about it. It was as if he had been cursed and was now being tortured ever since he had lost love.

Ethan reached his apartment building and ascended the stairs to the third floor. There was a lift in the building, but he always selected the stairs when available. He felt he didn't need to shortcut such an easy task as walking.

He arrived at his front door and took out a single key from his pocket to unlock it. He opened the door to reveal a very dim and dull living room. It was a two bedroom, one and a half bathroom apartment in which he stayed, but he only really took up his single bedroom. He would spend about an hour a day in the kitchen trying to make something that was fairly edible and he would use his bathroom for the usual business and to cut his own hair. The other bedroom, restroom, living room, and dining room were never used. He had no need for them. Any television show he wanted to watch could be downloaded onto his computer for viewing and any food he ate could comfortably be eaten while watching one of these programs. The apartment was usually dim because light could only go in through four windows; one being in Ethan's bedroom, which was enclosed most of the time because of habit, one being in the other bedroom, which was also closed because nothing was inside other than a bed with sheets and a blanket, one in the kitchen, and one in the living room, which had drapes to cover most of the light.

Also, every room other than Ethan's bedroom was quite bare; his simple nature didn't feel the need for furniture or decorations. He wouldn't even notice them if they were set up around his place.

Ethan walked into the apartment and straight to his room, just like every other day. He got to his desk where his computer sat and took off the massive headphones he wore while transiting. He flipped his computer on and chose a song from his collection of 100 gigabytes worth of music.

Music was a huge part of Ethan's life. He would always have music playing around him as long as the time was appropriate. It began the minute after he got out of bed in the morning and went on to just before falling asleep at night, and sometimes even past that. What he listened to depended mostly on his mood, but it was typically either a very emotional hardcore rock or a soothing, emotional, atmospheric mix of post rock. But he had almost every genre you could think about, from classic rock to gangsta rap to classical to R & B. He didn't have country music, though. No one likes country music.

At that particular time, Ethan scrolled down his collection to a group named port-royal to begin playing the epic triad of 'Flares pt. 1', 'Flares pt. 2', and 'Flares pt. 3'. During times when he would feel a bit lonelier and emptier than usual, these three songs were a good choice for him.

The songs are electronically mixed, with lots of ambient sounds coupled with sections of light, slow guitar riffs, piano riffs and artificial drum beats. There are very few bass beats in these particular songs, but the amount they do have is ample for the mood they wish to give off. The triad is about 23 minutes worth of music that may sound boring or repetitive to an unappreciative ear. Music of this genre needs a patient listener and an accepting mood to grasp how epic and meaningful these works of art are.

It may not have been the music itself in these songs that Ethan related to at that moment, but instead it may have been all the memories, feelings and emotions he felt every time he heard the musical story in the past. Every time Ethan would hear these songs, he would be reminded of different times of being alone in the past. Reminiscing of these events would only heighten his feeling of loneliness in the present. Some people visit friends or family to get their minds off boredom or being alone. Ethan is the opposite. It is as if he purposely wants to enhance the emptiness inside of him. Making a particular emotion an extreme one is like therapy for Ethan. But unfortunately, infinite sadness can't be healthy. And even more unfortunate, his lifestyle had set himself up for a catch 22. When he was alone, he would listen to music and inevitably link that loneliness to certain songs which would be heard again in the future, bringing back those memories. It was a kind of snowball effect with an unhappy sensation.

Ethan clicked the music on and briefly closed his eyes to begin his session. His most recent rejection had him feeling a bit down.

Now with music permeating the walls, Ethan walked to the kitchen to have a look inside his refrigerator. He saw a carton of orange juice, some tomatoes, a package of mushrooms and a carton of milk.

'Ugh, I really should go get some groceries,' he thought to himself. 'Let's have a look in the cupboard.'

Ethan opened the cupboard next to the refrigerator and found a package of pasta and a can of pasta sauce.

'Bingo. Looks like I got lunch.'

He didn't really care if he ate pasta twice already earlier in the week. It filled him up and kept him alive. Ethan didn't care much for gourmet food or even mediocre food.

As long as it got rid of his hunger, then it did its job well. He never understood people who would pay $200 for a steak or some exotic fish on the brink of extinction. The same satisfaction can come from a bowl of Frosted Flakes cereal. He didn't even need to heat his leftovers to enjoy them.

Ethan walked back to his bedroom. He unbuttoned his dress shirt, slipped it off and grabbed a plain white t-shirt to wear. That and a pair of jeans with sandals made up his wardrobe when he was not at work.

After getting into his more comfortable clothes, he flopped belly-first onto his bed and just lay and listened for a short while.

The emotional first bass beats from 'Flares pt. 1' boomed from the boxed subwoofer under Ethan's desk. The accompanying piano was perfectly coupled in to keep Ethan's head bobbing up and down to the sounds for about 30 seconds. Spurts of bass like these were cushioned with dreamy electronica.

Ethan lazed and his thoughts of Sara swarmed in his head. He thought about her so much. She was already a major part of his life and she didn't even know it. He lay, unmoving, imagining seeing her at work about an hour before. That and every moment with her were embedded in his memory. It was as if he had selective photographic memory and could recall every bit of detail about his time spent with Sara, but only Sara.

Ethan recalled the scent of cherry blossoms he smelled when he sat next to Sara in the office. He remembered the facial expression she had after reading the short poem he wrote for her. He saw that she truly appreciated and enjoyed receiving the token. Not only at that single instant, but every other nice gesture Ethan had done in the past for Sara did she show actual forms of happiness.

  The numerous times he had her favorite flowers – orchids – delivered to school during working hours for everyone to see had Sara on the edge of tears. The time Ethan made a scale model of the solar system, with the sun being a small statue of Sara, Earth being a small statue of Ethan and the other planets being other statues of what things Ethan wished the two would have together in the future. These included a dog, two daughters, a small shack to resemble their house, a moped for their transportation, a bowl of rice for their meals and little matching coffins to show they would be together until the end. Sara was amazed at the thought, time, and energy put into the wonderful gift. And even the time Ethan serenaded Sara at the office with a unique rendition of one of Ethan's favorite songs which was untitled from the album *...to Forever Embrace the Sun* by the band named skycamefalling brought her almost literally to her knees. She had always loved seeing just how much Ethan cared about her and her feelings.

  Ethan's eyes narrowed. He sat, contemplating past occurrences similar to the above and the way Sara would react to them.

  By that time, 'Flares pt. 2' continued where 'Flares pt. 1' had left off. A soft, clean electric guitar with lots of reverb began to repeat the same soothing riff over and over again. That same riff goes for over half of the nine minute song then gets converted to another similar one to finish off the remainder.

Ethan thought, 'She must truly like me for her to give off the responses that she has been.'

This thought lingered in his mind all the way until the seven minute mark of 'Flares pt. 2' came on, and trumpets blared.

'She has *got* to have some feelings for me.'

Ethan was analyzing and trying to convince himself of the possibility for his dream to come true.

"She's got to!" Ethan said aloud to himself, scrunching his eyebrows inward.

'Hmm, should I call her out on it?' Ethan went back to his thoughts. 'Should I message and tell her what I think and put a stop to all these shenanigans?'

'But what should I say? I don't know what to say.'

'What about if I start the message by saying, 'I know you have feelings for me'? How does that sound?' Ethan questioned himself.

'Hmm, I guess that's good. But then you need to add how you know this.'

'Okay, okay. How about I say, 'I know because of how you act every time we're together and every time I do something nice for you'?'

''Every time we're together'? I think you're getting too cocky. Dull it down a bit.'

'Okay, just, 'Every time I do something nice for you'.'

'That's better. Keep it simple. Next, you gotta reassure her that these feelings are okay to have, even though she has a boyfriend.'

'Okay, then I'll say, 'It's okay to have these feelings even though you have a boyfriend'.'

'Wow, you're a genius!' one voice exclaimed.

Ethan continued to brainstorm.

'That sounds okay, but I don't think you should mention her boyfriend. We want her to keep her mind on just the two of you.'

'Yeah, you're right. Okay, I'll take that part out. It'll just be 'It's okay to have these feelings'. Her boyfriend will be implied. She'll understand. She's a smart girl.'

'Okay, good. Hmm, I think next you should remind her how you feel, to let her know you still have these feelings.'

'Should I be subtle and gentle?'

'Hmm, you're trying to stop all the games and get right down to business, so I think you should be kinda direct with how you feel and what you want. I think you gotta almost demand.'

'Yikes. Okay, let me think for a second.'

Ethan's thoughts paused to have some thoughts.

'Okay, okay, how's this: 'You know that I fell in love with you long ago and that I will always love you. I want you to be with me, to stop playing with both of our emotions and fuse them together as one as we love each other for the rest of our lives'?'

''For the rest of our lives'? Is that too much?'

'Maybe. But I want her to know what I really think.'

'That'll do it. Sounds good to me,' Ethan admitted.

'Make it so,' Ethan demanded to himself in a Jean Luc Picard voice.

'Don't be scared about this. Just take out your phone and text her exactly what you have just said.'

Ethan froze. His hands weren't listening to the brain signals telling them to grab his phone. His hands and fingers were paralyzed from nervousness. Or was it something else? Had something fallen on his head? Were tranquilizer drugs slipped into his meal earlier? Was he having a stroke?

All the times Ethan was with Sara he was very calm and smooth when he spoke to her. He felt very comfortable around her. He never hesitated to tell her anything – even if it were something he thought Sara might not want to hear. Some guys freeze up in their actions or words when they are around beautiful girls. They may stutter or fidget around because butterflies flutter deep within them uncontrollably. Just like a 10 year old schoolboy, they would be on the border of vomiting from simply having a conversation with someone of the opposite sex.

But not Ethan. Ethan was very suave around girls – even the girl who made guest appearances in his dreams. In actuality, Ethan felt even more comfortable talking to girls than boys. He obviously wasn't gay, or even bisexual for that matter. He felt his thoughts were shared more commonly with those of females'. He enjoyed discussing intellectual topics and radical ideas and he came to find out it were females who were more receptive and contributing to these types of conversations. So Ethan had grown more and more accustomed to chat about his passionate – sometimes difficult – quandaries with girls.

It was the time *before* contacting or interacting with Sara that would turn Ethan into jelly. If he was about to meet her for lunch at school or show up at her office for any reason, he would become one of those fifth graders with swarms of insects flapping around in his stomach. He had yet to conquer that feeling. He learned long ago how to deal with it while in the presence of a female, but somehow he couldn't seem to modify the comfort to extend to the time before contact.

And moments like the one he was in at that time, on that afternoon, were especially worse. All of Ethan's hopes and dreams and feelings could be broken with a single reply to his message.

'Should I risk it?' he thought to himself. 'What if she tells me to fuck off and never wants to talk to me again?'

'Come on, really?' another voice in Ethan's head spoke up. 'Do you really think an innocent girl like that will say such things?'

'Well, I don't mean those exact words; but what if she tells me—'

'Dude! Shut up!' the second voice said sternly. 'You're just trying to stall. Pick up your damn phone and text her what we just talked about.'

'But what if she says no?!'

'Then she says no! At least you'll know and at least these silly games might finally come to an end.'

'You're right. I'm just going to pick up this phone and start texting.'

'That a boy. Make it happen.'

Ethan reached into his pocket for his phone. He took it out, held it up, and stared at it.

A minute passed.

'What the hell are you doing?' a voice asked softly. 'Start texting, numbnuts.'

'But what if—'

'Holy shit! Give me the fucking phone! I'll do it!'

Ethan's bodily functions were handed over to the aggressive voice.

'Alright, how'd it begin? 'I know you have...'' Ethan began to type out.

The Flares trio had already finished and the album with the same name kept rolling on to the last track, 'Stimmung'. A low key piano played through the computer speakers. It was a slow, melancholy riff, one that could make its way into a love story – but only after the main character had found out he had lost his love.

Realizing that song wasn't the best for his current situation, Ethan got up to change it mid-text.

He temporarily put his phone down and scrolled down his list of songs on his computer. He thought he needed something more lively and uplifting.

'Hmm... no... no... no...' he thought as he eyed different artists and songs.

More scrolling.

'Aha! This will do.'

Ethan double clicked to start the song 'I Fall So Far and I Fall So High' by artists The Timeout Drawer. They are an electronic/post rock group which plays emotional songs using guitars, drums, keyboards and mixers. Their songs can be described as depressing to energetic and hopeful. The song Ethan chose was one which reminded him to stay hopeful and positive and to remember things work out for the best. A perfect song for that instance.

He picked his phone back up and continued the text from where he left off.

'...rest of our lives.' He finished the message.

Again, he froze. The aggressiveness wore off. It was only a quick burst of energy. It was an imposter. It wasn't all ballsy like it made Ethan think. A fraud.

The voices came back.

'Are you sure you want to do this? Couldn't we just leave things the way they are?'

'Yeah, everything is fine just the way it is. Why change things and risk messing everything up?'

'Just continue being nice to her. She'll come around eventually.'

'You're both having fun. Just leave it alone.'

"No! Fuck this!" Ethan yelled out loud to himself and pressed the send button.

It was done. There was no turning back. You can't un-send something once the commitment was made. Time travel hadn't been invented yet, so he couldn't go back to just before pushing the button. The odds of phone lines being crossed and having his message pop up on a random phone was too high for it to even be considered as a way out this.

He could only watch as the status bar grew to its capacity. Once there, it was over. It would have been sent.

Any millisecond...

'It's still going. I can still throw my phone out the window and smash it before the message is sent.'

'Come on, now,' another logical voice started. 'You're a man of physics. You know all too well yourself that by the time the phone hits the concrete from the third floor, the message will have already gone through.'

'I don't know. Not necessarily. If I give the phone enough initial velocity, it should actually get there in time to stop this madness.'

'Or I could run into the kitchen real quick to get a hammer to smash the phone.'

'Why do I keep a hammer in the kitchen?' Ethan questioned himself.

'Nevermind that! What are we going to do?!'

The sound of a drop of water came from Ethan's phone. The message had been sent. Now there truly was nothing to do but wait for a response. To wait to see which way the rest of his life would turn out. To see what fate would do to Ethan. But he didn't believe in fate. To see what Sara's answer would do to Ethan. To find out if he would be alone for the rest of his life or be with the girl who he loved for the rest of his life. Apparently there was no in-between. Just these two extremes. Ethan really *did* turn into a ten year old boy before hearing an expected message from Sara.

All sorts of thoughts bounced in Ethan's head.

'Was the wording all right?'

'If she says no, what are you going to say back?'

'What if she gets the message when she's with her boyfriend? Do you think her answer will be influenced?'

'I never should have texted her. I should've just kept everything the way it is.'

'Do you think she's reading it now?'

'Did you spell everything correctly? Was all the grammar okay?'

'What should I do now?'

'Are you sure there's no way to un-send something?'

A few minutes had passed. Enough time for one of the saddest songs to come on Ethan's computer from the same album that brought the optimistic song. The song changed to 'This Narrow Room is World Enough'. It played very simple guitar riffs using hammer-ons, pull-offs, and slides, one guitar on top of another with light cymbals and snares. The saddest part, to Ethan, was toward the end of the song, when a heavy, deep bass introduced itself with an electronic backing and trumpet sounds. The extremely low sounds always reminded Ethan of the more depressed and lonesome times in his past. It was an unbelievable resonance and it amplified any similar mood.

Ethan's hand vibrated along with his phone and a short ring was heard. His heart jumped. It was a reply. He didn't look down to read it. He was too scared. It could be the beginning of a nightmare. He didn't want his demise to start just yet. He needed more time; more time to think. To think about what? Hadn't everything that could've been thought out been thought out already?

Indeed. It was time. No more lollygagging. He lifted his phone closer to his eyes and read the message.

Chapter Seven

'How can I think of baseball when I have these two basketball boobs bouncing back and forth in my face?!' Jaime thought to himself.

He continued to pound in and out of his customer, trying to hold back his orgasm. His face scrunched up as if he were being tortured by having scalding oil pour down his back. He normally didn't have the problem of giving up his seed prematurely, especially when it was his second different vagina that day. But he suffered having to have sex with two of the most beautiful girls he had ever seen in his life within the span of a few hours. The poor guy. He was showing so much will power. He was sweating profusely from holding back. It wasn't long before he would have to just let go.

The girl kept her hands on the sides of her enormous breasts and pushed to smash them into one another after every thrust from Jaime. She howled like a werewolf, in what Jaime thought could only be a forced feeling of passion. But it was all real. This mother of two was a hell of a screamer. All the neighborhood kids stopped their playtime outdoors to curiously listen to the yelps from inside 591 Blossom Way. Neighborhood moms' conversations were in brief stasis. They were disgusted to hear the screams from the 'slut's' house. It wasn't the first time they witnessed adultery from that girl.

All of the cries and yells and all that flesh and softness brought Jaime to a tipping point. He was about to explode.

"I can't hold it any longer! I'm going to cum!" Jaime exclaimed.

The door knob 10 feet away from the lovers jostled.

Two last pumps from Jaime.

"Aaaaaaarrrrrrrrgghhhhhhh!" he yelled with pleasure.

The front door swung open with the husband's arm attached to the knob.

Jaime pulled his cock out of the girl as his heart rhythm increased to almost the point of detonation. His surprised, wide-open eyes shot over to see the intruder.

The husband shouted, "What the fuck?!!!"

"Aaaaaaarrrrrrgghhhhhhhh!"

Jaime's cock pulsated with every squirt of sperm arching towards the woman's breasts. His penis needed no more stimulation. It was standing freely.

Jaime held his arms out as if he had just been caught robbing a convenience store. His penis bobbed up and down, squirting.

"Oh, fuck yeah!" the girl screamed out.

Sperm kept spewing.

"I can't stop it!" Jaime shouted to the husband. "Tell it to stop!"

Ounces and ounces leaked out like blood would do from a ruptured artery.

Still facing the husband, Jaime scrunched his face in a satisfying pain.

"Give it to me, baby!" the wife shrieked out, only making matters worse.

"Who the fuck are you?!" the angry husband said fiercely.

He was a pretty muscular guy. He lifted weights to keep in shape and his strong physique showed through his modern, gray business suit. He was the least bit happy to see another man discharging their juices all over his wife. His fists clenched, preparing for a battle. But he stood in the doorway, as if he were allowing Jaime to finish inseminating the luscious breasts of the woman. It was a long 20 seconds.

"Ahhhhh, fuck! That was awesome!" Jaime said loudly with a smile forming. He started to see how awkward and hilarious the situation was.

Jaime didn't mind how the husband outweighed him by about 60 pounds and how he was built like an MMA fighter. Jaime got his. He was satisfied. He really didn't care about any repercussions that could arise. But the less, the better.

"Baby," the woman said toward her husband, "it's not what it looks like. We were just fucking." She let out a small laugh and grin.

It was obvious to Jaime that wasn't the first time the girl had done something like what she had just done.

The man released his grip on the doorknob and started after Jaime.

In a flash, Jaime scooped up all of his clothes and ran toward the window that stood beside the front door, in an alcove. With a big smile on his face, he took two long strides and a leap on the third step. He flew at the window with his shoulder lowered like an NFL linebacker protecting his quarterback. Mid-flight, Jaime looked over to see the husband standing in awe as he watched Jaime fly like a superhero. Fuckman took care of his business and was now on his way out, still naked, showing the world his true identity. He was in full battle suit.

The woman did a partial sit-up to watch Jaime's escape plan. Her hair was a mess. It was strewn throughout her face, in clumps. She was a massive, elongated lake of sperm that stretched from her stomach to the indent below her throat.

Jaime's right shoulder was first to make contact with the window. It rolled forward, allowing his upper back to slide onto the glass. Next, his lower back, then his butt. Very soon after, the rest of his body. He had successfully shown the window was capable of sustaining all of Jaime's body weight being thrown at it after a giant leap. Jaime fell straight down onto the floor like his body was made of rubber.

"Dammit!" Jaime yelled out, more embarrassed than hurt.

The other two didn't say a word. They stood there watching as Jaime was reduced to nothing. Their faces were blank. The husband had lost his rage. The wife had lost her afterglow.

Jaime quickly arose from his downfall and raced out of the front door, running right past the man as if he weren't even there. Jaime still carried his clothes in hand and was still very much naked. He ran across the front lawn on the balls of his feet, afraid to step on something sharp or dangerous. His thin body made him look like a being from out of this world, and his tip-toeing didn't dull the impression.

Again, all the neighborhood women and children stood at arrest as Jaime crawled back into his delivery truck. He still carried a smile that reached from ear to ear. He was dying from laughter on the inside.

Jaime threw the key into the ignition and started up the delivery truck. He pulled away from the side of the street and headed for the main road to get back on the freeway. The cool breeze felt wonderful and was perfect to relieve his escapade. His delivery truck wasn't equipped with a door on the driver's side so to give the worker easy access in and out of the truck. All drivers to the left of Jaime's truck gawked as they observed him showing it all. The passersby were appalled, but Jaime was laughing. He couldn't get enough of the feeling. He loved moments like those.

He didn't bother to take the time to put on any of his clothes. He was taking a chance of being pulled over by any police officer and possibly being cited for indecent exposure or a similar charge. Police officers in California are quick to put an end to public nudity. They find it to be disruptive to public.

A text message buzzed in the glove compartment and just at that moment, Jaime realized he was going to be late for his dinner with his girlfriend, Stephanie.

"Awww, shit!" he exclaimed, his joyous mood now hindered.

He popped open the compartment and retrieved his phone.

'Hey baby. I got here early and I'll wait for you inside the waiting area,' the message read.

Jaime looked at the time displayed on the phone.

6:03.

'Shit! I got 30 minutes to get to Ontario from here,' he thought. 'Hold on tight. It's gonna be a quick ride...'

Jaime knew the streets of most of southern California quite well and he knew the 210 freeway going from Garden Grove to Ontario would be a parking lot. He was going to need to take the surface streets as much as possible to try to save some time. He wasn't really in a mood to have an argument with Stephanie, so he wanted to limit his tardiness to a minimum level.

Even in the busy traffic of the suburbs, Jaime was reaching 50 miles per hour. He was zooming through orange lights and narrowly missing pedestrians making their way across streets. His van almost tipped over on numerous occasions from the sharp turns Jaime was making. His nudity needed him to be inconspicuous, but his fear of Stephanie trumped that. But he couldn't show up to Spaghetti Heaven with his cock hanging out freely. He needed to start covering himself up.

Stop signs weren't stopping Jaime, but walls of cars from cross traffic did. He used those opportunities to slowly slip on one article of clothing at a time.

Californians don't use their horns while driving. They think it is rude. But Jaime put it to good use during that run through many cities. There probably would have been a trail of dead bodies had he not.

Chapter Eight

Astrid tossed her head all about her pillow, trying to find a spot free of tears. That entire afternoon was full of sobbing for her. She had sent numerous messages and calls to her boyfriend Ronnie, but had yet to receive an answer. She was devastated at the thought of losing her first love. People's first love is always the hardest to get over. Astrid didn't want to go through a 'getting over him' phase. She wanted to keep the man she loved.

It had been only a few hours, but she already missed holding Ronnie. His scent still lingered on Astrid's shirt and every inhale she made reminded her of what had occurred earlier that day. She saw the image of Ronnie dismounting her and leaving her behind replay in her head over and over. She rubbed her blood-shot eyes to clear away some moisture.

She let out a loud wail.

"Ronnie, answer your damn phone!"

An empty house heard her cry. She had never felt more alone.

Her house turned into an endless cave and she was now lost inside. She knew her cries were pointless and Ronnie ignoring her made her feel hopeless. The cave was getting darker and darker as she fell deeper inside. Colder, more narrow, less air. Her breathing got heavier. Her mind tricked itself into seeing every exhale in the imaginary freezing air. Her thoughts echoed. Her pulse raced. She needed a life line.

She picked up her phone to try one more time. She dialed Ronnie's number.

One ring.

Two rings.

Three rings.

Four rings.

Ronnie's voicemail prompt came onto the receiver.

Extremely disappointed, Astrid slowly lowered her phone and ended the call. She was completely defeated. She was better off dead at that moment in time. At least then she would not feel the heartbreak taking over her body.

Past memories of her and Ronnie together broke levies and began to flood her thoughts. All of the wonderful times they shared. All the wonderful emotions shared. They were once intertwined like shoelaces in their daily lives. They spent so much time together. How could the end of it all happen in a blink of an eye?

The doorbell of the house sounded. Astrid's eyes shot wide open.

'Ronnie?!' she asked herself.

She jumped out of her bed and dusted herself off, as if that would help get her composure back. She wiped her face with the bottom of her shirt. She shook her entire body to try to look as normal as possible, as quickly as possible.

Not wanting to keep Ronnie waiting, she hurried to the front door as soon as she thought her sadness was all wiped away.

She turned the knob and opened the front door.

"Hi, would you like to buy some delicious Girl Scout cookies?" a high pitched voice came from about three and a half feet off the ground.

Astrid let out a large sigh of dissatisfaction.

"Oh, I'm sorry, sweetie. Not right now. But if you promise to come back tomorrow, I promise to buy two boxes."

"Deal!" the cute salesgirl said excitedly with a smile.

The little girl's smile quickly faded when she squinted to have a better look at Astrid's red eyes.

"Are you okay?" the girl asked Astrid. "Your eyes don't look normal."

Astrid took a heavy blink and replied, "Yeah, I'm fine. I was, uh, just cutting some onions."

"Cutting some onions?" the Girl Scout asked curiously.

"Yeah, when some people cut onions, the onions make them cry."

With a confused look, the girl said, "Those onions sound mean."

Astrid gave a small laugh.

"Bye bye!" the little girl said. She turned and skipped away from Astrid's house.

Astrid turned and closed the door. But just before it fully shut, a quick two knocks sounded.

"Ronnie?!" Astrid said loudly.

She swung the door back open and saw a young man carrying some flyers standing on the doorstep.

"Hi, there," he said. "Is your mother or father home?"

"No. They stepped out for a minute."

"Awww, shucks! Okay, no problem. I'm from Gary's Sprinkler Service. Can you give your folks this flyer and ask them to call us if they ever need service?" The young man held out a flyer for Astrid to take.

"Yeah, yeah. Sure thing," Astrid replied and took the piece of glossy paper.

"Thanks! Have a nice evening!"

"Bye, now."

Astrid shut the door. She began to walk back to her cave when three more knocks on the front door had her running back.

She opened the door quickly and yelled out, "Ronnie?!"

Disappointed again, she stood looking at the neighbor boy, John.

"Oh, hi, John," Astrid said in another sigh.

"Hi, Astrid. Me and my sister hit a ball over the fence. Can you toss it back for us when you get a chance?"

"Yeah, no problem, Johnny."

"Thanks, Astrid!" John said and started to swiftly run back to his house.

Astrid headed for her backyard to retrieve the ball that went off course.

Three more knocks on the front door.

Astrid paused in her tracks.

She turned back around to answer the door, this time in no rush. She was tired of having her emotions played with.

With low hopes, she opened the door, yet again.

Surprised, she took in a deep breath.

"Molly!" she released her diaphragm. "Your brother was just here!"

"Really?" Johnny's sister asked.

"Yes. Are you here about the ball over the fence?" Astrid questioned.

"Yeah, can you throw it over for us?" she repeated the request with a big smile.

"Of course, Molly. Just give me a sec." Astrid closed the door and headed for the backyard.

The front doorknob jostled. This made Astrid's ear tingle with curiosity. Two seconds later, she heard, "Astrid?!"

She spun around, knowing the voice was that of Ronnie.

"Ronnie!" she yelled out again, this time in a slightly angered voice.

Astrid was thrilled to see Ronnie had returned, but she didn't want to show him. She didn't want him to know she was completely depressed and crying her eyes out for the past few hours. She didn't want to give him the satisfaction of knowing she would slip into a never ending hell if he ever left her. She wanted him to think she was angry with him more than ever before and that she wouldn't easily forgive him for leaving her stranded earlier. She wanted the apology of the century from him. She wanted to hear that he would never do that again in the future. But, of course, that was just what her facial expression and voice spoke.

Deep down, she was bursting with happiness. Her heart was beginning to reconstruct itself. Life was beginning to pump through her veins again. Her emotions were starting to shift to the lighter side of the spectrum, where bunnies jump to and fro in a wonderland made up entirely of pastel marshmallows. Her resurrection had begun.

Astrid stood with her hand on her waist to support her façade.

Ronnie walked up to her and said, "Look, baby. I'm sorry about what happened earlier." He held his hands and arms outward to begin his explanation.

"It was wrong of me to leave you all alone like that. I understand that you are not ready for sex and I truly respect your decision."

Astrid listened intently at the deliberation. So far, so good. It sounded like he was coming around to a reasonable understanding.

"You don't want to have sex yet, and I sure as hell don't want to force you to have sex with me," Ronnie continued. "Your first time should be a memorable one. It will be special. Obviously your first time can only happen once, so I understand how much it means to a girl."

'Not bad,' Astrid thought to herself. 'The deep apology should be near.' She kept listening.

"I know it's not very romantic to do it in a backyard and in a bench swing. It needs to be in a place where you feel much more comfortable and much more relaxed. We're not wild animals who can just fuck anywhere with others watching and listening to our squeals."

'Aww, he was doing so well. It sounded so scripted like a poet would do until that last remark.'

"I understand all of this. I know chicks are weird like that. And I also know that maybe I'm not the right kind of guy to give you what you need."

'Uh oh,' Astrid's heart began to beat faster as things started to turn for the worst. 'I don't like the sound of where this is going.'

"I dunno, Astrid. Maybe we should just break up."

'No! Don't say that. Go back to saying all those wonderful words of understanding and finish it off with 'I'm sorry and I love you.''

"I think maybe you and I are too different and are looking for two different things. And maybe we can't give each other what we want."

A tear trickled down Astrid's right cheek. Her angered attitude had been smashed and replaced with horror. Flashbacks of days spent with Ronnie twinkled through her mind again like the memories of childhood flash through a dying person's thoughts.

"So maybe it's for the best if we just go our separate ways," Ronnie concluded.

There was more than just a single tear running down Astrid's face then. It happened. The unthinkable had occurred. She would soon be in a spiral leading to a fissure, an emptiness that would envelope her whole.

Astrid didn't even retort. Those words she had witnessed were powerful enough to bring her into a state of shock. Her body was an upright cadaver. She was experiencing a rigor mortis where she stood. She wasn't even sure if her involuntary body functions were being processed. She didn't know what to do. She obviously didn't know what to say. So she only stood as small puddles of tears began to form on the floor between her two feet.

Ronnie also stood for a moment. He was waiting for some kind of acknowledgment or sign of life from Astrid. But it never came.

After about two minutes of silence and awkwardness, Ronnie turned and walked out on Astrid for the second time that day.

Evening slipped into night. Light to dark. Happiness to sadness. Love to heartbreak. Quite a sentimental experience for Astrid, that day had been.

Chapter Nine

Sara sat just feet away from her boyfriend John, but her thoughts were miles away. Ethan covered every brain cell she had free. She sat in a chair at her home's dinner table twirling her steamed vegetables with a pair of chopsticks she had cooked earlier for an afternoon snack. Her eyes followed the greens as they snaked around the small, round dinner plate in front of her. Her head slumped with her shoulders. She was upset she couldn't gather the courage to send Ethan a simple message to invite him to dinner so she could tell him how she felt.

Her feelings toward Ethan were no longer a mystery. If Ethan was the only thing she could think of – especially while being with John – then it must have been a true feeling of desire. It wasn't a crush. A crush has more lust and sexual want when compared to the feeling of love or likeness. Sara's emotions toward Ethan were stronger than any schoolgirl's crush.

"We really scored it big today at the office," John told Sara. He was oblivious to her remoteness at that time.

"We'll be able to buy ourselves a nice house very soon so we can start a family together when everything else is ready," he added.

Silence. Sara only heard a voice. She couldn't make out the words the voice wanted to share. She was too much in contemplation about something of greater value. Nothing could break her focused meditation.

"Sara? Are you listening to me?" John questioned. Silence. The voice was still scrambled.

"Sara, answer me!" John demanded with a louder tone.

It wasn't until a minute later when John slammed his palm on the dinner table that Sara snapped out of her fantasy. She shook her head back and forth and squeezed her eyes shut to get a grasp of reality.

The drinking water in the small cups that lay beyond the two's dinner plates rippled from the force of John's hand. Instead of just a silence, an eerie stillness followed.

Sara looked up from her downward gaze into John's eyes. But she couldn't keep her stare. Sara's eyes quickly looked away to a beautiful painted vase that rested on an end table, just outside the hallway separating the bedrooms of the house. Her observation ricocheted from the vase to pans hanging in the kitchen, then to the clear sliding door that led to her backyard. She fired her sight again across the room, this time to a painting in the hallway, then down to her vegetables, then back up again to the microwave in the kitchen. She was lost. She didn't know where to look. It was as if everything was brighter than a thousand suns and she would go blind if she looked at a single object for more than a split second. She definitely couldn't look at the bright white dwarf star named John.

"Sara," John repeated in a softer, calmer voice. "I said we'll be able to buy ourselves a big house pretty soon if things keep going well at the office.

John worked at an investment company that dealt with market transactions. His main specialty were day trades, which are the buying and selling of stocks in short periods of time, rather than giving the stocks ample time to fully mature or do the opposite. Day traders usually deal with high amounts of money because the small gains in the market in short time frames would be too insignificant of a profit if the initial investment were low.

Sara's head dipped back down. It was like she was about to get a verbal punishment from her father and she needed to hold her head in shame.

Silence.

"Are you going to respond in any way?" John made sure Sara heard every word.

Again, silence. Sara thought the situation was beyond repair and didn't want to speak or make sudden movements to agitate John even more.

He calmly placed his hands on the edge of the table and gave a slow, but hard push to bring his chair out from underneath the table. Keeping his movements steady, he rose up out of his chair and walked to the front door.

He placed his right hand on the doorknob and said, "I work so hard so we can build our lives together. But how can we be together if you don't even acknowledge that I'm here?"

John thought he was the victim. Sara thought she was the victim. Who was supposed to apologize to whom? Was an apology needed between them? Who would pursue whom? And how would they initiate any conversation? It was a strange situation, but it wasn't a rare one. Many couples go through similar occasions.

Sara got up from her meal with her head still hanging. She went over through the hallway and into her bedroom. Her legs kept stepping forward until her mattress prevented them from going any further. Like a falling domino, she collapsed down onto her soft bed littered with stuffed animals.

Sara's room was like that of an eight year old girl. She had posters of her favorite celebrities hung on each wall. She had a pink iMac computer on her desk with stickers of cartoon characters around the outside of the monitor. Stuffed animals were almost literally everywhere. Her bed was always made and she placed some animals on top and all around in a strategic method so they wouldn't be considered clutter by anyone else who saw them. Frills surrounded her window, which was always left so the sun could shine brightly through. Small toys and figurines were placed on her bedside tables, posing as if they were about to have photographs taken of them. Although she had collected many decorations and accessories over the years, her room was never a mess underneath it all.

Sara kept her head buried in a Spongebob doll. She thought she should try to wait everything out. She felt like staying out of destiny's way during this particular circumstance. She wanted things to fix themselves with fate's hands rather than her trying to meddle. Her eyes were wide open but could only see darkness.

Sara was alone. John left her. She didn't have the courage to contact Ethan earlier. Spongebob's shoulder was the only one to cry on at that time.

Destiny came ringing – or rather, Sara's phone did, in the form of a message.

Sara reached to her purse which sat on top of one pillow. She felt around until she touched the smooth leather of her bag. Her face was still smashed into Spongebob's. Without looking, she opened her purse with one hand and fished for her mobile phone. Once found, she brought it back to where her head lay.

She raised her head and pushed the button on the face of her phone to light it up and Ethan's name jumped out at her. Her upper body quickly jumped up to view the message more comfortably. She swept her finger across the touch screen to unveil the message from Ethan.

'I know you have feelings for me. I know this because of the way you act every time I do something nice for you. It's okay to have these feelings. You know that I fell in love with you long ago and that I will always love you. I want you to be with me; to stop playing with our emotions and fuse them together as one as we love each other for the rest of our lives.'

'哇塞 (wa sai),' Sara thought. 'He knows. He knows I like him. 哇塞.'

Her face gleamed red. She was embarrassed in front of her dolls. Her heart beat faster and faster and her breathing became heavier. Her revealed secret was equivalent to her initiating a relationship with a boy which was preposterous for a traditional Chinese girl. She was much too shy to do something like that on purpose.

'I need to calm down and relax,' she told herself.

She took deep breaths to steady herself.

'What should I say back to him? Should I play dumb and tell him that he doesn't know what he's talking about?'

'No, you can't do that!' a different voice denied the other. 'You should just tell him that he is 100% correct and you both should get together immediately.'

'Don't be too aggressive. Relax a little. You're talking nonsense.'

''Nonsense'? How is it 'nonsense'? It's exactly what you want him to know, right? You were going to message him something similar earlier, right?'

'Well, yes, but I can't just come out and say that. He'll think I'm insane.'

'So then what do you think you should tell him?'

'I should be more passive and lady-like.'

'But even he said himself that he wants a direct answer and to stop playing around with our feelings. He wants you to be straight-forward.'

'I don't think I can do that. It's not in me to say such things.'

'Do it,' the aggressive voice demanded.

'I can't,' the passive voice said in a whimper.

'Do it and do it now.'

'Okay, okay, look. *I'll* type it all out in the reply but *you* have to send it. Deal?'

'You're such a baby.'

Sara began to key in a reply.

'Here goes. I'm doing it. So now you're going to have to fulfill your part of the deal and send it once I'm finished.'

Sara punched in, 'You are 100% correct...'

Moments later the passive voice spoke up again, 'All finished. You're up next.'

In a flash Sara's finger pushed down on the send button. She immediately threw the phone down to the mattress and cupped her hands around her mouth in shock. It was as if her phone turned into a pile of snakes. She pushed herself back and stared in awe at what had just occurred. She couldn't believe she was being so open.

She couldn't move. Her body locked up. Her breathing sped up to keep with her increasing heart rate. Her elbows pressed against her upper body. The only sound in the room was that of her intense breathing. It seemed as if she would hyper-ventilate. She was like an eight year old boy about to board his first roller coaster.

Sara got up from her bed. She felt she needed to do something to keep busy and try to get the travesty she had just done out of her mind. She paced to her desk and picked up a figurine of Hello Kitty. She lifted it up towards her head to get a better look, then put it right back down. She spent more time ensuring the figure was in the exact same spot as when she got it than actually looking at it close up. Her hand bounced back and forth between tapping the plastic doll and rubbing her chin to jog her memory of the space the doll occupied before.

Sara did an about-face like a military soldier and went to her door to close it. She then jumped to her window to have a peek outside.

Outside, a small breeze was picking up. Tree limbs swayed and let out a low swashing sound like waves gently coming onto the shore. In the brief few seconds Sara spent looking out her window, she could see a flock of small birds flying in formation high above the tree line. Rays from the sun penetrated through the vacant spaces in the trees to create a kaleidoscope on the street underneath. Clouds in the sky moved quickly, in perfect harmony with the flow of a falling leaf in the wind. No children were playing in the streets, no cars were moving, no one was out fetching their mail nor were there any artificial noises during those few seconds that ended up being a short calming heaven for Sara. She only witnessed Nature and she suddenly felt at ease.

Sara turned herself around and took a deep breath. Her nerves were slowing and her jitters were ceasing. She closed her eyes and relaxed. Everything was much better at that moment. Her worries vanished. Her breathing went back to normal. She opened her eyes.

The pile of snakes hissed at her with a new text message. Sara's heart leapt and went back into panic mode. Her muscles tightened and sweat poured on her skin. Her hands cupped her mouth again, her eyes widened. She froze.

'Oh, my god!' Sara thought. 'What have I done?!' she hollered at herself recalling the message she had sent to Ethan.

'Oh, my. What do I do now?!'

'You go over to your phone and see what he replied with,' a different voice pointed out the obvious.

'I can't just go over there and read the message. I need to prepare myself. What if he says 'no, I don't want to see you' or what if he says 'haha, I was just joking'? I need to get ready for answers like those.'

'How can you even think he would reply with something like that? I mean, you did read his initial message and you know how wonderfully he treats you, right? There's no way he would say such things!'

'Maybe you're right… So he's going to say that he wants to get together! Oh, my! I need to prepare myself for *that* answer then!'

'What are you talking about 'prepare myself'? All you are going to do is read the message he sent to your phone.'

'It's not just any message! This message will be the beginning of something great. Do you think I'm dressed okay?'

''Dressed okay'?!?! What the heck?! All you're doing is reading a message on your phone!!'

'Hmmm, do you think I'm overreacting?'

'Just a little, dear. Now get over there and take a look at what he said.'

'O… o… okay…' the voice stuttered.

Sara slowly began to move her right foot forward, her hands still clasped over her mouth. Her foot lifted straight up then moved forward three inches and quickly back down again. She could almost hear the carpeting rise as she gently and ever-so-slowly let up her left foot from the ground. It rose one inch. Two inches. Two and a quarter. Back down to two inches. Up to two and a half inches. Then her foot slammed back down.

'No. I can't do it. I'm not ready,' she told herself.

'Of course you are, sweetie. Just take a deep breath and relax. Nothing bad will happen. You must trust me.'

'I don't know. What if something bad *does* happen?'

'Remember? We already went over this. His reply will be something you want to see.'

Sara hesitantly took her right hand off from her mouth and very slowly reached for her bed. Her feet, this time, weren't going to be the preferred mode of travel. She imagined hot lava filling every piece of her bedroom floor except for the small area under her feet. Sara's upper body leaned forward as her hand reached the bed sheet. At that time, she took her left hand from her mouth and lifted her left knee to place on the bed. Slower than a tortoise, her knee reached the safety of the bedding and she began to repeat the same action for her right leg. She made very little sound, as if she were trying to not wake a sleeping ogre that would devour her if seen.

A spring inside her mattress squeaked as tension built up from the pressure of Sara's weight. This sound made her go even more slowly. Her face still showed a shocked expression. She was now on all fours, staring at her phone and centimetering in. Her mouth opened and the inside began to quickly dry up. Sara could hear her own heart beat heavily. Closer and closer she got. She took irregular gulps due to the slight irritation in her throat from lack of moisture. Similar effects were happening to her eyes.

She kept pushing herself in onto the phone until her face was practically touching it. She could notice her nostrils slightly flailing out and in with her gaze downward at the phone. Condensation formed on the screen of her mobile with each breath. The phone's light was off, so she could only imagine what lay hidden inside. It was now as if she had just stumbled across an unknown species of salamander and she was the first human being to examine such a unique structure of its pointed snout.

Her arm swung around and she placed her fingers over the phone, the same way one would do when showing off a small photo, not wanting to get any fingerprints on the face of the glossy paper. Her middle finger rested on a button on top of the phone. Pressing down would reveal the message. But was she ready to seal her fate?

She rolled her eyes up and thought.

'Is this it? Am I going to push the button?'

'Yes. It is time. Don't be afraid, my child. I'm right here by your side. Go on and push the button of destiny.'

Sara gently pressed down her middle finger. The pressure between the finger and the switch grew until a soft click sounded.

Sara smiled.

Chapter Ten

Jaime ran into Spaghetti Heaven and reached Stephanie in the waiting room at 6:45 – only 15 minutes late.

Stephanie sat with her legs and arms crossed. She didn't have a very happy face on. She was upset and she wasn't afraid to show Jaime. She wanted him to know he kept her waiting and she wanted at least an apology for his momentary absence.

"You're late," she stated.

"Babe, I'm like 15 minutes late," Jaime replied. "There's so much traffic at this time. I was coming from Pasadena."

Stephanie's anger started to fade. There was no way for her to stay mad at Jaime and they both knew that. Jaime always knew a reasonable explanation and apology always put Stephanie's mind at ease.

Jaime was panting from his short sprint from the parking lot to the restaurant, mostly because the only exercise he ever got was when he made love to another woman. But this time, it was also because he wanted to show his girlfriend he tried his best to get there on time. Truth be said, he reached Ontario in damn good time.

"You're right. I wasn't waiting too long, anyway," Stephanie admitted. "Come on, the girl told me she'd have a table ready for us by the time you got here."

Stephanie got up from her seat and took Jaime's arm. They walked to the host stand and had a server see them to a table for two.

"So how was your day, babe?" Jaime asked. He wanted to try to keep the conversation topic on her that entire evening. He didn't want to expose his recent sexcapades.

"It was good. One of the girls showed me how to blend a fade into guys' hair. It looked easy at first, but it's actually really hard."

"Did you get to try it yourself? Or did you just watch another stylist do it?"

"I watched at first, then tried it for myself," Stephanie explained. "It was cool because there was this guy who was already in there to get a fade and he was totally fine with me experimenting on his hair."

"What?! Really?" Jaime asked in shock. "You didn't mess his hair up?"

"Nah. See, what happened was Bonnie started on one side of the guy's head to show me. But she started the fade really low. Then I tried it out and failed miserably. But Bonnie was there to fix it. The guy was really cool about it."

"Nice. So you'll be able to cut my hair soon, huh?"

"Not for free. You gotta pay me extra."

"Pay you extra? Then I'll just go to your work and have Bonnie cut it for me for free."

"Fine, go to Bonnie. But she won't give you special treatment like I would."

"Hmm, what kind of special treatment is that?"

A big smile came across Stephanie's face and she squinted slightly in her right eye to give Jaime 'the signal'.

"Oh! *That* special treatment!" Jaime blurted out.

"Yes, that special treatment…"

Jaime gave a cocky look at Stephanie and said, "I dunno, I think with the right tip she'd be willing to give special treatment."

"You sicko! She's like 50 years old!"

Jaime raised his head and eyes in a pretend showing of ecstasy. "Ahh, yeah. Fifty years of experience. She could probably do things to me that I have only watched on tele—"

"Whatever, you nasty boy! You know you can't resist *my* pussy. There's no way you would choose her old, crusty, smelly knife wound over mine!"

"I dunno… Crust *is* my favorite part of a pizza. I love old French fries. And the right smell can make me harder than high school chemistry. So you've got some pretty tough competition there," Jaime said with a smile.

"Alright, fine. You can go have her. If that's what you really want…"

"I want, I want!"

"Whatever, jerk."

A short moment of silence passed. Jaime got comfortable in his chair. He slouched down more than usual. After all, it was a busy day for him.

"Tired? Had a busy day today?" Stephanie asked.

"Yeah, I'm beat."

"How many deliveries did you have?"

"Only three. All around Pasadena."

Just then, Jaime realized he said the wrong thing. He spoke the truth. What was he thinking? Nothing good could come from the truth.

"Only three? All around Pasadena?" Stephanie gave a confused but curious look. "Then why so tired?"

"Yeah, it must be the heat. There's no air conditioning in that truck, ya know. I sweated my ass off in there."

"Yeah, I bet it's like a sauna inside," Stephanie gave quick sympathy, then tried to dig deeper by asking, "But why were you late getting here?"

Jaime knew he was in trouble. It always began in this same fashion. His adulteries were always exposed by Stephanie getting inside Jaime's mind and forcing the truth out of him. He was usually left with no other choice. It would either be to come clean with the truth or fake a heart attack. Ambulances are so expensive...

"I told you why I was late. There's so much traffic at this time."

"I agree. But you went to work today at eleven 'o clock. How could've it taken you so long to take care of three packages?" The mathematics weren't adding up correctly in Stephanie's mind.

Jaime started to get uneasy. He knew he needed to think fast to create some explanations or stories. He rose a little out of his slouch.

"Yeah, babe. I had a long lunch with a friend after my first delivery."

Only a small piece of that was true. That's what Jaime wanted. The truth would get him kicked to the curb again. So he began to hide from it. He was starting to do well. Back on track.

"Oh, a friend? Who?"

Even though Jaime saw this question coming from a mile away, he still didn't bother to prepare an answer. He was now caught off-guard.

"Yeah, uh, my friend Lucas."

Lucas was the first name that popped into Jaime's brain. He wasn't even thinking of an actual friend – or person for that matter. Before he replied, the thought of one of Jaime's favorite childhood candies came to him for some odd reason. The candy was a sweet powder form of chili and sugar and was quite popular amongst the Hispanic community. The powder came in a small, plastic , cylindrical container, proportional to about a fifth the size of a soda can and labeled with the name 'Lucas'.

"Lucas? Who's Lucas?"

Stephanie knew just about all of Jaime's friends and family. But apparently, one by the name of Lucas had slipped by her knowledge.

A female server walked up to the table where Jaime and Stephanie were seated and said, "Hi, you two! How are you? Can I get you started with some drinks?"

Jaime was sure relieved to have the tension broken.

"Ppsssshhhh," he let out in a big exhale. "Yeah, of course you—"

"No, could you please come back in five minutes?" Stephanie politely asked. She felt she was on to something and needed the momentum.

"Absolutely! Take your time," the server said then left.

Stephanie had a serious glare at Jaime. She asked again, "So, who's Lucas?"

"Oh, Lucas? Lucas is this guy I met while at work. I delivered something to his home a while back and we got to know one another."

"Sure. Can you tell me about him?" Stephanie asked in a calm voice. She knew to ask a question that would cover all basics instead of asking about Lucas' home, family, lifestyle, friends or personal affects individually. Stephanie knew if she did that, Jaime would have more time to think about his lie. Yes, she knew Jaime well enough by that time. She was already aware he was lying.

"Yeah, of course I can tell you about him," Jaime said. Instead of immediately explaining, he gave Stephanie that filler statement so he could gather his thoughts and lies to try to form a cohesive story that would be believable.

"Umm, he's this guy I met in Pico Rivera like a couple months ago," Jaime started. "We talked about DJing when I first met him. He DJ's for some house parties and stuff and I was trying to see what kind of music he does or see if he has played at any bigger venues or events."

Jaime once experimented with DJ equipment when he was in his teens. He got to the point where he was able to mix out a good 30-minute set of hip hop, but he never took it serious enough to make it more than just a hobby.

"And, I dunno, what exactly do you want to know about him?" Jaime asked to try to get some more ideas.

"Just tell me more about him," Stephanie calmly demanded.

"Well, I don't know too much about him. He's just some guy I met."

Wrong answer. Boys always have trouble keeping the same story. If this were a game of spades, Stephanie was about to trump Jaime.

"So you don't know much about this guy who you spent a long lunch with. You can see why I don't believe you, yes? Why don't you just tell me the truth? Lucas is a girl, isn't she?"

That last assumption from Stephanie was a mistake. She led with a small spade. It could go either way, to her favor or against. But she never should have brought upon that circumstance. She was in the clear and just needed Jaime to reveal everything, but now he had an assumption that he could rebuke.

Jaime instead went for a stall.

"Look, babe," Jaime slyly pointed to another table far to the right. "That guy over there must have been stood up. He's dressed up all nice and everything with flowers but the chick is missing."

Stephanie looked to where Jaime pointed and saw a young man dressed in a collared, tight blue dress shirt with white pinstripes. He sat alone with a glass of water in front of him, which was almost empty. He held a small bouquet of pink roses in his hand, not bothering to lay them on the table. The man had a blank face and looked infinitely forward.

'The poor guy got stood up,' Stephanie thought to herself and gave a small sympathetic pout of her chin towards the man.

'The lucky guy got stood up. He won't have to be in the same situation as me,' Jaime jokingly thought to himself. But truthfully, Jaime – or anyone – would hate to be in the same situation as that man.

Stephanie turned back toward Jaime. Her pout died away back to seriousness. "So, what's the deal? Tell me the truth," she said.

Jaime turned back to Stephanie. His face gave a look of defeat. He took a deep breath and said, "Okay. I'll tell you the truth. One of the deliveries today was to a girl's home. She was really pretty and she invited me in for a glass of wine. I took it as her way of tipping me, so I couldn't refuse."

There was a pause.

Stephanie continued the story for Jaime, "...and you fucked her..."

Jaime had been caught again. He was nabbed by detective Stephanie Guzman. She was the best at solving these types of situations. But hell, Jaime didn't make it too difficult for her to figure it all out.

"Look, babe," Jaime said in a comforting voice. But a person who had just been cheated on doesn't need a comforting voice. They need a chainsaw.

"Don't 'babe' me, Jaime. You've done it again! How the hell can you cheat on me again?! Do I mean absolutely nothing to you?! Don't you give the slightest fuck about my feelings?! You're fuckin' unbelievable!"

Stephanie stood quickly and her chair toppled over behind her.

"I can't stay here to listen to anymore of this shit, Jaime! I'm outta here! You need to stay away from me with your cheatin' ass!"

"Stephanie, hold on! Wait!" Jaime pleaded. His words fell on deaf ears. She didn't want to hear anything else from Jaime that day.

You would think Jaime would have learned to be loyal to his girlfriend after so many times of being caught. You would think he would have learned of the terrible feeling he bestowed unto Stephanie after each time she caught him. And you would think Jaime wouldn't ever want to purposely make her feel that way. Well, he doesn't really do it on purpose. He doesn't really want Stephanie to grow that massive pit in her stomach and that pain in her lower heart. It is almost as if Jaime was blinded every time he ran into a situation where he had a possibility of having sex with another girl. Jaime didn't look into the future to see his girlfriend's heart shatter when she found out. His girlfriend was the last thing on his mind during those times. Hell, not even that. His girlfriend was far behind the last thing on his mind during those moments. The priority was getting satisfaction. He needed to fulfill that craving, that want, that *need*.

That is one of the differences between people who cheat and people who do not. Cheaters feel they *need* to have sex and can't control those urges when an opportunity arises. Those who are loyal find ways to control this *want*. The inability to fight this desire can be associated with having an actual psychological problem because there is nothing this person can do, really. They are trapped going down a one-way street, but they don't *feel* trapped. Rather, they feel liberated, completed once the activity is accomplished.

Chapter Eleven

Ethan jumped and threw his arms into the air, almost smashing his knuckles against the ceiling of his bedroom.

"Woooo!!!" he let out a deafening cry of excitement. "She said yes, she said yes! I'm going out with Sara tonight because she said yes!"

It was one of the happiest moments in Ethan's life. He was emitting all the adrenaline in his blood through song, dance and air guitar. He was a pinball, bouncing throughout his apartment, singing praises.

Ethan ran into his kitchen and grabbed a spatula. He held it up to his mouth and used it as a microphone to sing, "Joy to the world! I'm going out with Sara!"

With one hand on the microphone and one hand skyward, Ethan was living out two of his fantasies – being a rock star and having the girl of his dreams. Nothing could stop him right then and there. He was the drug addict hyped up on PCP. He was the contestant during the announcement of her first place prize of a beauty contest. He was the soldier coming home after a year on the front lines. He was the worker giving his boss 'the bird' on his way out of a job he despised. He was the sickly patient about to be cured of all ailments. He was all of these put together, multiplied by ten, on the last day before the end of the world, while holding a round, rainbow colored lollipop.

"Joy to the world! I'm going out with Sara!"

Ethan raised his wrist to read a watch that wasn't even there.

"Hmmm, it's about another two hours until I meet Sara… The bus takes a long time to get up to the restaurant…" Ethan thought out loud to himself. "I should probably get ready now. I don't want to keep her waiting."

Ethan threw his microphone away to the side and hurried back to his room. He opened his closet door to choose a nice shirt to wear for the occasion. All of his dress shirts were the same style; they only differed in color and slightly by material. Ethan's fingers flipped through the hung shirts and pulled out a blue one with white pinstripes going down. He held it up and said, "Ah, yes. This should suffice!"

Like a ballerina, Ethan hopped and skipped to the side of his bed and plugged in an iron that lay on his nightstand. He carefully laid out the shirt to get it ready to free it of all wrinkles.

While the iron heated, Ethan spun over to his computer to play a song called 'Happiness by the Kilowatt' by Alexisonfire – very fitting for the moment. He twirled back to begin ironing his shirt.

"So this… is… continuous happiness…" Ethan sang along with Alexisonfire and his movements went along with the unique drum beat.

Ethan pressed on the iron to spray bursts of water on the shirt. He wanted to make sure to get all evidence of wrinkles taken away. He wanted to look the best he could for that upcoming event. Ethan didn't have an ironing board to use, but the layers of sheets on his bed created enough padding and support.

After a few minutes of tending to his shirt, Ethan jumped into his shower to scrub every orifice of his body. He paid extra attention that time – more than any other. Every piece of his body would smell of spring fields from the body wash he used. It wasn't until he was fully satisfied and fully cleansed that Ethan shut off his shower tap and continued his freshening up with a shave.

Even after stopping to pick up a half dozen pink roses to give to Sara, Ethan still arrived 30 minutes early for his date. He stepped down from bus number 365 and took a short three minute walk to the restaurant to wait for his rendezvous with the girl he loved.

Ethan walked into the restaurant and to the hostess stand.

"Hi," Ethan greeted the young hostess behind the podium. "I'm meeting someone very, very special tonight. I was wondering if you can show me to an area where there is the least lighting. I have two candles I want to set up for ambiance, if that's okay."

The girl let out an "Ooooohhhhhh" of envy and continued with, "That's so sweet! Your girlfriend is so lucky to have someone like you!"

She picked up a pair of menus and told Ethan, "I know where to put you two. I'll put you at the table furthest away from others and it's also the dimmest."

"That sounds perfect, thank you," Ethan said with a smile.

The hostess walked ahead of Ethan and led him to a great location for a couple and then she asked, "How does this look?"

"This will be wonderful. Thank you, again."

"Sure thing! Oh, and would you like me to grab you something to put those flowers in while you two dine?"

"No, that won't be necessary. But thanks for being so helpful," Ethan said.

Ethan sat down and the girl laid both menus onto the table.

"My name is Ethan and my date tonight is Sara. Could you please send her my way once she arrives?"

"Absolutely. And if there's anything else I can do for you to help you out, don't hesitate to let me know."

Ethan made himself comfortable in his chair to endure a short wait more easily. Not wanting to damage the beautiful flowers in his hands, he kept them there and didn't dare lay them down. He looked around the restaurant and noticed it getting busy. It was, after all, dinner time for most. He saw couples and families being sat down to begin their evening out.

Ethan noticed one couple, in their 20's, waiting for their meals to arrive. Their eyes were wide and their faces luminous with smirks. They were having a nice time together, talking it up. Ethan could hear every detail.

The young man Ethan saw said to his partner, "No way! There's no way she could've done that!"

Almost laughing, the girl responded with, "I'm dead serious! Why and how could I make up a story like that?!"

Unfortunately Ethan missed the details of the beginning of the story.

"Oh, my god! I can't believe she did such a thing!" the boy said.

"I know, me either! So, see, it was a good thing you weren't there…"

"Hmm, I don't know. I think I kinda wanted to see that happen."

Ethan looked on as the couple laughed out loud. He felt the excitement and happiness the two shared. That didn't happen very often for Ethan. He would usually be at a restaurant eating his dinner alone, spaced out in his own world and absent from all other reality. He would usually contemplate his loneliness and wallow in his own personal drought. His heart would cry out for another soul to share time with him. He would fantasize of having someone – anyone – sit across from him out of a whim and start a conversation. His fantasy person didn't even need to be female. During those dark times of loneliness, all Ethan wished for was another human being to realize his existence.

But at that time, Ethan didn't feel alone. In a matter of moments, his heart would be satisfied with the ultimate guest.

A waiter reached Ethan's table. He was a tall, young man with dirty blond hair. He wore all black, just like the other employees at that establishment. He was very energetic and excited to be there.

"Hi, sir! How are you this evening?!" he asked Ethan.

"I'm doing great, thank you," Ethan replied.

"Are you waiting for the rest of your party to arrive?"

"Yes, I am."

"Okay, not a problem. Can I get you anything in the meantime? Maybe a glass of water or some other drink?"

"Yes. A glass of water would be nice, thank you."

"Not a problem. I'll have that out for you in a jiffy."

The waiter smiled and went to fetch the water.

Ethan opened the menu which lay in front of him with his single free hand. He glanced at the delicious photos and colorful writing down below, but he didn't actually read or pay much attention. His nervousness had begun. He could feel his body starting to warm up and knew it would soon begin to perspire. Mild shakes were spurting in his hands, they being already dampened. Ethan tried to focus his eyes on the menu below, but they were already doing a good job of bouncing around, unable to rest on a particular object. Ethan's right leg jumped on the ball of its foot. His breaths deepened and his bladder felt weak.

The sounds of laughter from a few tables over caught Ethan's attention and he shot his head in that direction. A family of four was all laughing, most likely from a joke the father had just told.

Ethan's head recoiled back to his left when his waiter startled him with his arrival, water in hand.

"Oh, sorry about that sir," the waiter said. "Didn't mean to scare ya."

"Not at all," Ethan said, releasing a large inhale. "Thank you for the water."

Ethan quickly took a sip through the straw.

"Sure. Can I get you anything else while you wait?"

"No, this will be fine for now, thank you."

"No problem. If anything should arise, you just let me know," the waiter said and then left.

Without a watch around his wrist, Ethan could only guess the time was about 5:45, 15 minutes until Sara's scheduled arrival. He was getting very antsy, but not because of the wait. It was because of his anxiety. He couldn't sit still. He was fidgeting around in his seat. His armpits were now sweating and his hands were clammy. He was like a nervous boy about to go on stage in front of a large audience for a spelling bee.

Ethan needed to keep his mind busy. Again, his eyes wandered, this time in search for something to entertain himself for a while. He caught sight of the bartender towards the entrance of the restaurant. She was a big girl. She wasn't fat, but just big. Ethan figured she was about five feet ten inches tall and must have weighed about 150 pounds. She had dyed black hair that streamed down to her breasts and flipped outward at the tips. She could almost be mistaken for a circus worker because of all the makeup she wore. It was caked on. Probably to hide her early wrinkles on her 35 year old skin. Ethan could tell she knew her way around her bar from the smooth pours and relaxed smile she had on. She had probably been doing that kind of work for 15 years.

Ethan's attention turned to a customer of the bartender. It was an older gentleman, maybe about 65 years old. He looked quite spry and energetic for his age. He wasn't even sitting in his barstool, but instead standing behind it and talking loudly to anyone who would listen to him. Ethan couldn't hear anything the old man was saying, but he imagined the man spitting out corny jokes. The man would laugh every now and again, but he would be the only one. Others around him would smile at best. But that didn't stop the old man from continuing his stand up routine.

A waitress walked next to Ethan's table.

"Excuse me. Where are the restrooms?" Ethan asked.

The waitress stopped and pointed to a corner of the room and replied, "They're right down that way."

"Great. Thank you."

Ethan thought getting some 'fresh air' in the restroom would clear his mind and take up some time before his dream would manifest itself.

After doing his business in a urinal, Ethan washed his one hand and splashed some water on his face. He looked at his reflection in the mirror and verified his clothes were in order and there were no smudges on his face. Then he dried his hand through his bristly, short hair and went back to his seat.

Once seated, Ethan's legs bounced as if they were pieces of popcorn kernels being heated. He rested his free hand on his knee to make sure his leg wouldn't topple the table. But then Ethan quickly shot out his arm and lightly grazed it up against a passing waiter.

"Excuse me. Do you have the time?" Ethan asked the wait staff.

"Yes, I do," the waiter looked down to his watch. "Uhh, let's see... it's a couple minutes past six o' clock."

Ethan's eyebrows rose almost unnoticeably. "Great, thank you," he said.

The waiter smiled and walked away.

''A couple minutes past six o' clock',' Ethan repeated in his mind. 'That means she could be here at any moment now.'

Ethan's eyes widened from nervousness. 'She could even be coming through the door right now! Or, better yet, she could be steps away from this table! Oh, my!'

Ethan sat up straight in his chair and looked forward as if he were looking at something a thousand miles away. He had his free left hand resting motionless on the table and his other held Sara's roses as vertical as possible. If Sara really was only steps away, she would see a man who appeared fully disciplined – maybe too disciplined to the point of robotic. Ethan's breathing even slowed significantly.

Customers walking by looked at Ethan as if he were a museum piece. Although Ethan just wanted to give a good first impression for Sara on the first date, he, too, had realized he looked strange. So he shook the stone from his skin and tried to loosen up.

Ethan had been on first dates before, but they were never of this magnitude. The majority were after a few online conversations and they were hardly more than a first meeting of new friends. That's all most websites can offer, anyway. Ethan would browse photos on dating websites on those especially lonely nights. He wouldn't even give the written profile a chance unless the photo passed his initial test. Once in the user-submitted written material, if Ethan found a nugget he related to, he would send a message giving a brief introduction about himself, sparing most pertinent information needed in a relationship. He didn't want to waste too much time or seem too desperate. And because of that, his message would only be semi-serious, at best. For the most part, it would be difficult to discern Ethan's messages from spam messages that litter email boxes. Ethan, himself, would be surprised to see a reply from something that took him seconds to compose. But that is the usual mindset on sites like those. And when the galactic alignment occurred to sprout a physical meeting from one of these charades, Ethan would put just as much preparation into one of these 'dates' as he puts into styling his shaved hair.

But this. This was different. Instead of going in completely unprepared, he went in full force and ready to impress.

All Ethan needed was his guest to arrive...

Ethan's phone vibrated from an incoming text message and awoke him from his empty daydream. He gave his eyes a heavy blink to refocus them. He reached into his left pocket and grabbed his phone.

Ethan read the text message that was posted, 'I'm really sorry I didn't go tonight, Ethan. I found out John bought a home for the two of us and I think it's best if I stay with him. I'm really sorry.'

Ethan saw the name 'Sara' written above the message. He also noticed the time: 20:36.

Life and energy slipped away. Ethan's already slowed movements mimicked those of a sloth. He obviously should have seen the message coming, but he was unable to face reality. I guess he thought she could've been a couple hours late.

Ethan put his elbow up onto the table and rested his head in the palm of his hand. His head was locked down and his eyes would look directly at the table below if they weren't raised up to view a blurry world which lay outside the boundary of his lenses. The only movement was from his breathing. His body inflated slightly from the inhales and deflated with each rhythmic exhale. Ethan's eyelids came down heavily for a moment and went back up in no rush. His gaze continued off into oblivion and his mind followed. He was a conch shell without a host.

Time lapsed and Ethan found himself ten minutes in the future. The only changes that had happened in Ethan's world were that of a clock's hands. His were still holding the head and flowers.

Then, as if life was starting anew within Ethan, his eyes broke their stare and fled right, only to see a cloudy pillar. Regardless, it was an improvement. Ethan's head stooped lower, neither his neck or arm able to cope with the weight of sadness, and the whites of his eyes became bigger. They began to follow any movement in their vicinity, picking up figures of people walking, scratching, laughing, and cleaning. One person after another stepped alongside Ethan, giving him a strange look before they were out of sight.

Ethan's face was blank. He had no expression; he emitted no emotion. He kept it all inside. It wasn't his exterior that cried and withered. It was his very core of being which ached. He was churning on the inside. Not from hatred. Not from disappointment. Not from disgust. He was in devastation. All hope had been abandoned.

Ethan didn't have much in life. He paid full rent for a half-occupied apartment. He had a few tailored shirts to look presentable at work. He had maybe one good friend. He had a bus card with about nine dollars on it. He had a cell phone with the most basic talk plan. All of his material things in life could fit into a single suitcase with room to spare. He relied on his confidence and charm to get through each day. That's all he had.

But at that moment, while sitting alone at Spaghetti Heaven, he lost the little he did have. He felt his chance for true happiness eluded him that night and would remain at a distance he would never reach.

Chapter Twelve

Jaime pushed the glass doors of Spaghetti Heaven open with enough force to have them shoot back once entirely breached. He was closing the gap between him and his girlfriend Stephanie. She wasn't too happy after finding out Jaime had once again cheated on her. She stormed out of the restaurant immediately after hearing the bad news, not even having placed a drink order inside. She got a head start to the foot chase when Jaime sat in his chair contemplating what to do after he had been exposed. He was unsure about how much time to give his girlfriend to calm down before he tried talking to her again. She was an unstable volcano looming over a suspecting village.

It took a couple of seconds after Jaime reached the patio outside the restaurant to realize how wondrous spring evenings were in southern California. Spaghetti Heaven sat in northern Ontario, very close to the San Bernardino Mountains. They towered over most of the Inland Valley and gave off a cool blue haze that evening. One would see snow capped above only during the brief mid-winter air, but it was not needed to create a beautiful contrast against the radiant last glows of the sun squeezing themselves through streams of soft clouds. The bright oranges in the west faded to deep reds then to bold purples and ultimately to the relaxing blues in the east. Even amateur photographers could create masterpieces in southern California.

Jaime picked up his pace to reach Stephanie just before she unlocked the door to her dated Honda Civic. He swung her around and began to try reconciliation.

"Baby, please listen to what I have to say," Jaime begged.

Stephanie folded her arms across her chest and turned her head and sight away from Jaime. Traces of tears were reflecting light from a nearby street lamppost.

"Baby, I'm really truly sorry about this. My emotions were out of control this afternoon and I'm sorry that I couldn't get a hold of them. Stephanie, I love you more than anything else in this world and I'm sorry I hurt you again tonight."

Stephanie looked at Jaime and gave him a mean face.

"I know you may not believe me," Jaime continued. "But you truly mean the world to me. And I honestly never intend to hurt you. But I think the reason is because I have a problem. And I want us to try to push through these hard times and try to fix this problem together."

The first step is admitting the problem…

"Jaime, I've forgiven you time and time again. If you haven't learned how to control yourself already, then how do you think you will learn to do so in the future?"

"Babe, I know it sounds ludicrous, but you are going to have to trust me on this. I'm giving you my word that I'm going to try with all of my energy and power to not let something like this happen again."

Jaime was starting to see more and more of Stephanie's eyes. She was letting up and was getting ready to come around with forgiveness yet again.

"Jaime, the reason I wanted to have dinner with you tonight was to let you know that I'm pregnant again."

A shock went into Jaime's entire body. This same news had come to him twice before, but a person can never get used to that kind of information.

"And I want to keep it this time," Stephanie added. "I don't want to let this one go. I think it's time for the both of us to grow up and take responsibility for the things we do. And that especially goes for you. If you truly love me, then show me by taking care of me and our baby and never letting this shit that happened today ever happen again in the future."

Jaime only heard about three of the words which were just spoken. It looked as if he was paying attention to Stephanie, but she threw him a curve ball. His body was all there, but his psyche was unbalanced. What Stephanie had just told Jaime would be the turning point in his life. He knew it right away. As soon as she said she was pregnant, that was the trigger – the trigger that would skyrocket his new life and new way of thinking. He knew it was time to stop messing around now. A flash of his family life flickered in his thoughts and he knew this cheating needed to stop. Jaime grew up ten years during those few seconds.

"Okay?" Stephanie asked Jaime sharply.

Jaime scrunched his eyes closed and shook his head like a dog trying to dry his coat of hair.

"Yeah, baby. Of course. I'm going to be here to take care of you and our family. I'm not going to fuck around anymore. I promise."

Chapter Thirteen

The night air was cool. The temperature difference in southern California between day and night could be 30 degrees Fahrenheit, especially during spring or autumn. Only crickets could be heard throughout the residential roads of Chino Hills at that late hour of midnight – even on a Friday night. Most residents flocked to more exciting locations found around that region like Los Angeles or Hollywood or even down to San Diego. The air was still and slightly peculiar. The moon shone brightly, making the orange streetlights seem dimmer than they already were.

Astrid walked down Rolling Ridge Drive that night. She was better off outside rather than sleeplessly tossing around in her bed. Her steps were slow, but evenly spaced. She thought she was walking without a definite location in mind, but her subconscious had her going to a specific spot. She was actually heading for Ronnie's house and she didn't realize it.

'How could I just let him walk out the door like that?' Astrid asked herself, remembering hours earlier when Ronnie broke up with her.

'He waited for you to say something back to him, to say that things would be different. To say you'd give him what he wanted. He gave you a chance, but you were too scared to take it. And that's why you're all alone tonight. Good job.'

Astrid kicked a rock that lay on the sidewalk. She kept her head down. Her sadness overwhelmed her. Tears would trickle sporadically, when she could no longer control the melancholy. She tried her best to keep her whimpers to be nearly silent, so she could avoid alerting any guard dogs and causing unwanted attention. She could feel her heart bleeding and pumping harder to cope with the trauma. She hadn't eaten a thing ever since her lunch at school that day, but a growing, swirling mass in her stomach gave her enough reason to keep her fast. Her arms were crossed around her chest to mimic the sensation of a soothing embrace, but the only one she longed for was that of Ronnie's.

She reached a familiar mailbox which resembled a small barn house. Astrid recalled a time a few months earlier when she slipped in a romantic poem every day for seven days a week before Valentine's Day. She did her best to always keep Ronnie interested in her and cute gestures like that worked great.

A tear ran quickly down Astrid's face and onto the sidewalk where she stood. Her recent memory was too emotional for her. She gave strong sniffs to keep her nose from dripping. Her breathing became stifled. She was about to break down into a full sob when the front door to the house which she sat in front of opened.

A yellow glow radiated outward as if the house were a jack-o-lantern. Astrid saw a tall, thin silhouette walking out of Ronnie's house. It surely wasn't Ronnie, himself. The body structure was too feminine to be his, and the shadow of streaming long hair was a definite giveaway.

Astrid's stomach dropped. She was about to jump out of an airplane without a parachute to slow her fall.

'Who could that be coming out of Ronnie's house?' she thought. 'She's too small to be Ronnie's mom and Ronnie doesn't have a sister...'

She didn't want to admit to herself the reality. She needed to find a different explanation. She didn't want to believe.

Astrid did her best to hide behind the brick base of the mailbox. She squatted down and wiped away her teary remnants and watched as two figures now made themselves visible in the doorway.

The second was a bit fatter than the first but Astrid only needed to see the way it moved to know it was Ronnie.

The girl turned to face Ronnie and positioned herself so the light from within the house couldn't catch her. Astrid could now recognize the girl from school. Astrid knew her by the name of Roxy, and Astrid knew she was one of the prettiest girls in school. The girl would always dress in small outfits, showing off her round body parts. She had blonde hair and had one-of-a-kind green eyes. The girl hung out with the popular crowd at school and many boys loved her.

"Son of a bitch," Astrid cursed to herself in a whisper. "That son of a bitch dumped me for that son of a bitch."

As angry as Astrid wanted to be at Ronnie, her sadness overpowered all other feelings. At that time, she felt like she lost everything. Even though Ronnie dumped her earlier, it wasn't until she actually saw him with another girl that she realized the depth of the idea. She was truly alone then. Right then and there, she became a singularity. It was just Astrid now.

The two silhouettes got closer together. They became one. Ronnie not only wrapped his arms around his guest, but he wrapped his lips around her, too. It was a long, wet kiss. Tongues were being swapped and saliva ran wild in a controlled chaos. Heads were twisting. Ronnie had a hand in Roxy's hair and gently pulled on it to guide when he wanted to turn his head the other direction. His other hand rested around the side of the girl's breast, occasionally moving in to catch a feel of its entirety.

Astrid continued to watch from afar. Her eyes dimmed to slivers. She took a deep inhale. She felt a strangeness inside of her. Her anger and even sadness vanished in a blink of an eye. The blood inside of Astrid began filling up with energy, adrenaline. Her eyebrows tensed downward. Seeing Ronnie kiss another girl flipped the bipolar switch inside of Astrid. She thought she would be able to calmly and rationally watch the sham at Ronnie's doorstep, but she was afraid she couldn't go on much longer. The relaxed and mellow girl next door Astrid thought she was was about to erupt with anything but tranquility.

Astrid's hands clenched into fists and she rose from her squat. Her face showed the viciousness of a tiger protecting a recent kill. She was in full tiger suit.

The two at the door were still interlocked with their eyes closed. Their world shrunk to only encompass the two of them.

Astrid began to confidently and smartly walk toward Ronnie and Roxy. Her gaze was locked on the floozy hanging off of Ronnie. Astrid tightened her fists.

Ronnie's eyes opened from the sound of a knuckle cracking in his front lawn. He let out a gasp and let his partner go.

"Astrid!" Ronnie yelled in shock. "What are you doing here?"

With Ronnie's eyes just barely going beyond Roxy's, Roxy thought he was talking to her and she gave a confused look.

"What?" Roxy asked. "What's wrong with you?"

A moment later a strong hand grabbed onto Roxy's right shoulder and swung her around, away from Ronnie.

"Get your fuckin' hands off of him!" Astrid commanded. "He's *my* boyfriend and you're just a slut!"

Even Astrid didn't know what the hell was happening to her. She had never been so demanding or forceful. She turned in to the wild animal her suit resembled after seeing Ronnie with this other girl. Astrid even knew the words she spoke weren't logical. She was fully aware Ronnie had let her go earlier, but this super strength wanted nothing to do with logic. It was only there to get what it wanted.

Roxy quickly slipped into *her* tiger suit and gave a menacing look to Astrid.

"And who the hell do you think *you* are, bitch?!" Roxy yelled.

"I'm Ronnie's girlfriend, dumb whore! Get your hands off him!"

Ronnie jumped between the two girls.

"Whoa, whoa! Settle down, girls!" he said. He pushed open his arms to keep distance between the cats.

"Fuck you, little girl! Go back home!" Roxy screamed out to Astrid.

Dogs started barking at the sound of all the commotion. Some house lights came on, signaling spectators.

Seeing that Roxy wasn't going to back down easily, Astrid got a little scared. Her mean look faded really fast.

"Ronnie, tell this girl to leave," Astrid said, now about to cry. "Tell her that I'm your girlfriend. Tell her I love you and you love me. Tell her the truth."

There was silence.

Ronnie stood, still with his arms held out sideways, with a pretty girl on each end. His head was low. He contemplated. One part of him was happy to experience the taste and sensation of another girl. He thought it was wonderful to add this variety into his life. He felt he would be able to relive moments like that over and over again if he were single – holding, feeling, kissing, and smelling a different girl over and over again. He felt almost invincible.

But another part of him *did* love Astrid. Seeing her take initiative and finding him that night was a big turn on for him. It showed how much she really cared and loved him. It showed what she was capable of doing when faced with a loss of a loved one. To Ronnie, Astrid proved she truly loved him that night.

Ronnie turned to Roxy and said, "Maybe it's best if you just go."

"You're going to dump me for this little girl?! What is she, a freshman?!"

"Don't worry about her," Ronnie said to Roxy. "All you need to know is that I love her and I'm going to be with her forever."

Behind Ronnie, Astrid's face was one big smile. Her eyes let tears stream out. Her hands came up to try to hold in her cries.

"What the fuck ever," Roxy said to Ronnie and pushed him aside with one arm. "Get the fuck out of my way. You don't realize what you're passing up, buddy."

Roxy stormed off to her house four blocks away.

Ronnie faced Astrid and gave her a massive embrace. He took her back as his girlfriend after the very short fling with Roxy.

Astrid had her chin resting on Ronnie's shoulder. She sobbed more than ever before. She was so happy to feel Ronnie again, to be in his arms again.

That night, while enveloped in Ronnie, she vowed to do her best to never let Ronnie go ever again. She wanted to stay by his side for eternity. She decided to change herself to try to be more receptive of her boyfriend. She wanted to show him she would be more open. Besides, she didn't want to be the culprit again in the future.

But was Astrid the culprit? She was just hours away from being cheated on. Ronnie wasted very little time after he decided to go separate ways from Astrid a few hours earlier. It was as if he had Roxy already lined up and waiting for him to make the announcement. I know some people think dating or seeing other people after a break up is good therapy, but there are usually days – if not, months – of separation time in between – a time of actual grieving, of sadness, of reflection. But this was not true for Ronnie. While Astrid was turning her mattress into a waterbed, Ronnie was feeling up another girl. So, in essence, Astrid was taking Ronnie back just as a wife would take her cheating husband back.

Couples all over the world have the idea of cheating being immoral or wrong. The major religions, social views and even marriage institutions claim this concept of being true, even though humans are one of an almost literal handful of animals that practice monogamy. You read 'scandals' involving adultery committed by celebrities or officials in magazines and newspapers and watch soap opera divas' hearts break when they walk into a room to find their boyfriend's lips coalescing with another female's. Cheating is both subconsciously and consciously built into people as being bad and 'sinful'. And I'm sure anyone who has been cheated on can back up these claims – especially with their feelings heavily biased by the above. But if cheating is so socially unacceptable, why do many of the victims time and time again take back these fiends of all fiends?

Astrid was a pretty girl. Some bring up the notion of spouses or girlfriends or boyfriends who take their partners back after they had recently cheated do so because the former may be too unattractive to find another mate. These victims would rather forgive and repress rather than go through the trouble of making themselves over to put themselves up in the social showcase again. But this factor was not true for Astrid. She may have lacked a sliver of confidence, but doesn't everybody? And if you think you don't, then you have a different problem.

Traditional values have been known to keep a couple together after adultery. These values say it is better to keep the same partner no matter what happens between the two. One who courts with many different partners or who separates and gets together with another frequently may be seen as a harlot or whore. Or others may think there is something wrong, either mentally or physically, with a person who has had many different partners. So to avoid these assumptions by their peers, a traditional minded person may want to keep their original partner, through thick and thin. That's what love is, isn't it? The traditional mindset believes in eternal love.

So what could possibly be the reason one would accept a cheating partner? I believe a person who has cheated in the past is fully capable and susceptible to repeat the same action in the future. If that person was unable to control themselves the first time, what must change in order for them to change? The answer to this may be overlooked by a dependant partner opening their arms of forgiveness. These people could feel the need to have someone by their side and could possibly feel helpless when alone. This helplessness creates fear and the fear drives drastic decisions. But that dependence could be a more complicated situation and one that cannot be controlled. An example could be a mother with young children. The mother could devote all her time to the care and upbringing of her children. But if the father of the children is the only source of income for the young family and he decides to cheat, the mother's decision could be heavily predisposed by her dependence on her partner's help and support for their children.

And surely age can play a huge role in taking back a cheater or not. A person who is older may feel many reasons for not wanting to expose themselves back onto the dating scene. A lack of confidence, energy or time could be a determining factor brought with age. So continuing any relationship they may have could be the best option for them.

Regardless, in a society which condemns disloyalty yet floods the media with teasers and the concept of beauty as power, many victims of infidelity will always find a reason to move on with their partner.

Astrid did.

Chapter Fourteen

Ethan walked into McDonald's fast food restaurant. A long bus ride had him listening to the third song of The Fall of Efrafa's *Elil LP*, 'For El Ahrairah to Cry'. Ethan was in a mood for epic deep music. With a three song LP, averaging 21 minutes a song, it was a good choice.

Ethan's head couldn't find the strength to stay upright. He walked down the path clear of tables and chairs to reach the front counter. It was only him, his music, and his thoughts until then.

He reached opposite a lively young girl, surely still in high school. With a big smile, she asked Ethan for his order.

"Yeah, can I just have a regular cheeseburger and Coke," Ethan told the girl.

"Absolutely! Can I get you fries with that?" she asked.

Ethan stared down at the counter top and reached into his back pocket to get his wallet. He didn't ignore the girl's question; it just never breached Ethan's mind.

The girl with the name tag 'Jenny' gave Ethan only a couple seconds to answer before asking, "Is that for here or to go?"

Ethan pulled around his wallet and opened it. He got out a ten dollar bill and placed it on the counter. His fingertips stayed on the bill, as if doing so would prevent it from flying away from a freak gust of wind or from a thief snatching it up.

Jenny decided for Ethan. "Okay, I'll set you up with a tray so you can dine in."

She finished up the order and said, "That'll be $2.77."

Jenny grabbed the ten dollar bill and completed the transaction.

It wasn't long for Ethan's food to show up in front of him. He took the tray and found a table of two seats to rest in. He sat down and looked up. He saw a young mother, maybe about 22 years old, with her daughter, about three years old. They were smiling and the daughter was giggling over something unknown to Ethan. It looked like the little girl was joyously and loudly telling her mother some things, but the sounds didn't penetrate Ethan's big headphones. The little girl stomping her feet in excitement and the voice of the mother talking to the girl, probably asking to try not to disturb others was like a silent movie. Every slight detail went unheard – the movement of chairs, the rustling of French fries in their boxes, the slurping of drinks, the crackling of bags brought from other nearby stores. Ethan couldn't hear any of it underneath the deep guitar riffs sounding in his ears.

An old couple caught Ethan's attention. They sat to the right. From Ethan's guesses, he would say they were in their 60's and had been married for decades. They slowly chewed on their food – chicken sandwiches – without saying a word to one another. Their faces were blank and most people would think the lack of expression told a similar story. But not to Ethan. He looked intently at the two and imagined them living an exciting life together. He imagined the couple traveling to faraway places at every chance they got and experiencing life happily together. Ethan could see them resting on foreign beaches, climbing mountains, riding bicycles through countrysides, skiing down slopes and sailing seas. But most importantly, Ethan saw them creating everlasting memories and building a relationship and love that was unprecedented. The blank faces weren't that of boredom or unhappiness; they were that of fulfillment and understanding. Those two lovers knew just about everything about one another. They loved one another for many years and built a relationship that is rare during these recent times. What Ethan saw was genuine love. True love. It doesn't get any better than that.

Ethan smiled with envy in their direction. He was happy for them, but he also wanted to experience that feeling for himself. Seeing their old, worn faces made Ethan fast forward his own life to that age and to imagine himself alone even then. How sad and depressing that would be. Failure. Failure would be the only description of that situation to Ethan.

A tear gathered in his eye. Ethan shot his head down at his tray to hide if the tear happened to stream over his cheek. He picked up a napkin and wadded it up in case of the emergency. He opened his eyes wide to try to diffuse the moisture. He took deep inhales to relax his body. He didn't wipe at his eye so as to not attract any attention to it.

Ethan partially unwrapped his cheeseburger and took a small bite. He looked up to test if the tear would trickle. He was in the clear for the time being.

Beyond the young mother and daughter, Ethan saw a couple in their early 20's. It was puppy love between the two. The girl was feeding French fries to the boy and the boy was trying to stuff a double-decker hamburger in the girl's mouth. They laughed and smiled. Their eyes showed the beginning stages of love. They were happy to have found one another. They were mutually in good hands and care. Even a simple meal for this young couple was an amazingly good time for the two.

Time slowed as Ethan watched the two laugh and play in silence. The silence made him feel even more alone. Everyone in the restaurant could hear what everyone else was doing. But not Ethan. A large portion of the outside world was muted. He would almost always have his music in his ears throughout his day. It was rare for Ethan to hear birds singing, cars rumbling by, children's laughter, people talking, shopping carts strolling through supermarkets, wind blowing, dogs barking, voices through intercoms, doors slamming, sirens blaring, objects falling onto the floor, footsteps on tile, water dripping, etcetera. If any of those happened during Ethan's day, he was a mile away and could only see them occur and not hear them. He shut himself off from the rest of the world. It wasn't intentional. I mean, who wouldn't want to hear a child's laughter? But it was just the way Ethan lived his life which made him so alone.

He had very little interaction with people outside of his workplace. He only spoke to people who he absolutely needed to. He seldom left his apartment in the first place. Ethan entertained himself at home most of the time, through television, the internet and his music. He was one stop away from being a recluse.

Ever since Ethan began living in solitude, he learned to satisfy his hunger with simple meals like instant noodles, cereal, pasta or something with eggs. Going beyond these dishes would be a special occasion for Ethan. And he didn't mind the lack of variation. Well, he did *mind*. He just didn't do anything about it. Ethan hated hearing about colleagues gorging on feasts during the holiday season – especially when they would ask Ethan what *he* had eaten. Hatred shifted to embarrassment when he replied with 'noodles'. Of course, you may think all he needed to do was lie to his colleague. But that's easier said than done for Ethan. He had a strong belief against lying. So as for dining, Ethan would usually find himself eating alone while watching an episode of *Gilligan's Island* he had seen time and time again. Only if he were on the verge of becoming ill at the thought of pasta would he leave his solace to eat at a fast food or casual dine in restaurant.

There really wasn't anything else that would get Ethan out of his home, other than work. His acquaintances would have to give him an offer he couldn't refuse to get together with one of them for a night out. He felt very comfortable at home.

Ethan began noticing others giving him strange looks. But Ethan understood why and this was something that happened time and time again. It was usually one of a few different things that caused others to stare at Ethan. The most obvious were the massive speakers that enveloped Ethan's ears. People were used to seeing the small ear buds sitting just outside the ear canal. But Ethan preferred quality sound instead of looking 'normal'.

Another obvious oddity to society would be Ethan sitting by himself. He got more looks from this when he was at casual dine in places. He would be the only one who was unaccompanied by another. It is unusual for a person to go out by themselves.

Beyond that, people would take a slightly closer look and deem Ethan's everyday attire as too casual. His white t-shirts that others would wear as undershirts would have a small hole or two in them from overuse. They would be clean and white, just with extra eyelets. His plain jeans that most likely came from a thrift store were not perfect, either. But what really made people take a second glance were the close-to-a-decade-old pair of Chuck Taylor Converse shoes. Those shoes were a mess. They were once black, but faded to gray long ago. Discoloration was the least of the issues, though. They had holes, dirt, no traction, original laces, scrapes and the insides were coming out. The smallest puddle of water would seep through and wet Ethan's socks. But he didn't care. They were comfortable. And they didn't smell. Hell, how could they smell? They had plenty of holes to air out.

And if it weren't any of the above that made people stare at Ethan, then it would have been a reciprocation of what he was doing. Ethan would find himself examining couples or small families to see if he could figure out how he could join the club. He would watch other people's actions and reactions to find common factors. He thought he could learn from them and hoped to someday apply those teachings to a relationship of his own. He would sometimes make weird faces to others as if he were saying, 'Hmm, how did that guy end up with a beautiful girl like that?' or 'She can't possibly like what he is doing'. And that's what usually got the attention of others.

Ethan looked to the left and saw another young couple. It was as if everyone around him had a special someone with them. They were sitting side by side in a booth. They held one another and were chatting it up. They were both smiling and having a good time. They had every reason to be. They each had someone there to keep them company, to hold, to look into their eyes, to share emotion, to share themselves, to know the other cares about the other, to simply have another human being in their minds. The concept is so simple yet so important. It can bring such happiness or such ruin. It can separate the sane from the psychotic. Ethan was on the threshold of being accepted to the institution of white walls.

Ethan was now staring at the young couple. His mind ventured off.

'Why is it so difficult for me to find someone like that?' Ethan thought. 'What exactly is it that I am doing wrong? I thought I was nice, respectful, caring, loyal and all those things a decent human being looks for in a partner...'

Ethan *was* all of those wonderful things. He was privileged to have had a great upbringing by parents who were strict enough to enforce good morals, customs and beliefs, but not too strict to engrain fear or contempt towards them. Ethan's father, Rudy, passively taught him to always respect and cherish women through his actions toward his own wife. Rudy never put down his wife, Belle; he never yelled at her, scolded her, hit her or showed hatred at her. He always held the door open for her, let her express her opinions, sat only after she had done so, went along with her outlandish suggestions, including painting the inside of their house pink. Rudy loved Belle and his caring, thoughtful and sweet gestures made it obvious. Ethan was constantly around this admiration and learned to treat all women this way.

Rudy was an extremely loyal man. He never even thought about cheating on Belle or leaving her. They had been married for over 30 years and there was nothing that would have come between them. Rudy even stayed loyal to products and brand names. When he found something he likes, it would be his for the rest of his life.

He was also a very intelligent man. Growing up, Ethan never heard the words 'I don't know' come from his father. Whether it was a family problem, a road trip obstacle or a homework difficulty, Rudy always had an answer. And the answer usually turned out to be the correct one, not just a shot in the dark. Rudy understood the importance of having an education and was the only one in his family of eight to graduate from a university with a degree. But he didn't stop there. He was always informed of the current events and activities of modern society. Reading and watching the news every day made sure of this.

By now it may seem as if Ethan got all his training from his father. This is not true, but Ethan did look up to his father more so than his mother. That was a common occurrence for young boys. But all it took for Ethan to learn was to simply be around his wonderful parents.

'Does my breath stink? Is it because I'm too ugly? I do kind of look like a gargoyle, don't I?' Ethan asked himself. But he couldn't be further from the truth.

'Is it because I shave my head? Is it because I'm too thin? Is it because of the strange music I listen to? Is it the clothes I wear?'

He may have been on to something with the clothes.

'How could she choose him over me?' Ethan thought, referring to Sara rejecting him for John.

'I would treat her like a princess and she knows it. She knows I would treat her better than her boyfriend treats her, so why did she choose him? Does money and material really have that much of an impact on people? Is it really more important than happiness and being with someone who you know is the right one? It can't be. There's no way.'

The concept boggled Ethan's mind. He never put more value into money than needed. To him, all money was was a piece of paper with pictures on it. Money has no value. It lacks value. It is a printed form stating debt is owed by someone somewhere. I guess by definition debt is value, but it is on the wrong side of the zero on a number line. Ethan despised the faulty system so he only went along with what he needed to.

Ethan turned his head back to his tray. He emptied his mind. He kept his eyes on the wrapper that surrounded his cheeseburger. The orange lettering caught his attention, but it wasn't much attention. Ethan was passively linking one of the most depressed times of his life to yet another song. Although his eyes were focused, his mind was completely void of any thought. He was done. He didn't want to think anymore. He wanted to just throw everything away, to surrender his crusade of finding a girl to love. To surrender all things related to this search. Ethan raised the white flag.

He sat motionless like a dead stump in a forest. Life was still going on all around him, but it didn't exist to Ethan. He would catch the sight of a leg or two walk by in his peripheral vision, but he was so out of reality, the images would not manifest themselves into a thought. The only sounds reaching the inside of his ear were that of his music. He didn't move an inch. If he died right then and there, no one would know or even care. It would take days for someone to speak up about the foul smelling, decomposing mass sitting in McDonald's.

Without Ethan realizing, an hour and a half had gone by. He still looked downward at his meal with a single bite taken from the hamburger patty. His drink was beaded with condensation. He had a blank face, without emotion or thoughts.

Nonchalantly and unnoticeable, Ethan got up from his chair. He walked out of the restaurant and to the bus stop.

After waiting about 15 minutes for the bus to arrive, Ethan stepped in and sat amongst one other person. Underneath the bright white lights that lined the major streets of Chino Hills, Ethan stooped low in the plastic chair

and calmly waited to get back to his single occupant, two
bedroom apartment.